best kind of

AWKWARD

BECCA SEYMOUR

—— RAINBOW TREE PUBLISHING ——

BEST KIND OF AWKWARD

A SMALL-TOWN MM ROMANCE

COLLIER'S CREEK
BOOK ONE

BECCA SEYMOUR

RAINBOW TREE PUBLISHING

ALSO BY BECCA SEYMOUR

Zone Defense

No Take Backs | No More Secrets | No Wrong Moves | No Backing Down

Fast Break

Rules, Schmules! | Facts, Smacts! | Regular Smegular! | Easy, Schmeasy!

True-Blue

Let Me Show You | I've Got You | Becoming Us | Thinking It Over | Always For You | It's Not You | Our First & Last | Next For Us

Outback Boys

Stumble | Bounce | Wobble

Fangs & Felons

Thicker Than Water | Weaker Than Instinct | Brighter Than Fear

Stand-Alone Contemporary

Not Used To Cute | High Alert | Realigned | Amalgamated | Under the Blazing Stars | Best Kind of Awkward

COVER DESIGN: Rhys at Ethereal Designs

EDITORS: Hot Tree™ Editing

E-BOOK ISBN: 978-1-922679-66-6

PAPERBACK ISBN: 978-1-922679-67-3

CHAPTER ONE
COLTON

"Run it again." I hold back my wince as Maloney and Tennyson collide. Again. Both kids have two left feet, but rather than calling them out, I wait as patiently as possible for them to run the drill for the seventeenth time.

Unless these two kids are struck by lightning that gives them superpowers, the other kids on the team are going to seriously have their work cut out for them.

There's a screech of basketball shoes and a duet of grunts, and the boys who are making me seriously reconsider why I allowed myself to be talked into coaching the under twelves youth team fall to the court floor.

"Okay." Clamping down my sigh, I jog on over to

the boys, who are giggling and rubbing their shoulders. I'm grateful they're finding this funny and aren't crying. Plus, there's no sign of blood, so I'll take it as a win. "The two of you up." They jump to their feet, pushing against each other, still snickering like, well, the eleven-year-old kids they are. "What's going on? What are you struggling with?"

It's one of the simplest basketball plays ever. Sure, Maloney and Tennyson haven't played a lick of ball in their lives, but neither have Evans or Tucker. Now, those kids have a natural talent that's a joy to watch. While I've been coaching since I was fresh out of college more than a decade ago, it's still a hard pill to swallow when some players just don't have what it takes.

Not a chance I'll give up on them, though.

If they make just one well-timed pass, get one ball through the hoop, I'll burn my throat raw from how hard I'll celebrate with them.

Not that I blame these kids' lack of skill at all. Collier's Creek is a football town.

Not only that, it's one of those salt-of-the-earth places where I'm already learning that everyone knows everyone—and usually their business. Sure, there's a tourist element to Collier's Creek, usually folks seeking out quaint-town living. I get it. It's super picturesque. But despite the haul of tourists over the summer (and I've been warned to expect more in fall when it's the annual Jake Day festival), it's a real tight-knit community.

I'm just hoping I can find my place here.

I took up a science teacher position at the start of the academic year, and Principal Kendall all but salivated when he discovered I was a pro at youth basketball coaching. Add in that I spent a summer at Montview Academy, the place to be for elite college basketball players who are practically a shoo-in for going pro, and he scrambled to get a team started—thinking of the future when these kids would be joining high school.

There's nothing like high hopes and forward planning.

Something I'm all too familiar with, since most of my life was built around the dream of playing professionally. A navicular stress fracture put a stop to those hopes, though. So, science teacher it was while I usually got my basketball fix from coaching high school kids.

And honestly, I have no regrets. Life's been known to throw too much shit in my direction for me to waste time wondering what could have been.

Staying optimistic takes work, but I try my hardest to find the joy in life.

That's not so hard with the eager kids surrounding me.

"Evans, Tucker."

The kids are before me a beat later, bright-eyed and eager to please. "Yes, Coach?" they say in unison, and I barely hold back my lip twitch.

"Demonstrate zig-zag slides for me."

The boys run into position, and I call Maloney and Tennyson to stand at my side. "You boys are fast," I say, peering down at my players, who both have two left feet. "I know you can handle this drill. You just need to be aware of your space." I aim a reassuring smile their way. "Watch the drop step." I point it out to make sure they're looking in the right direction. The fact that Maloney and Tennyson keep colliding, despite the whole drill not even being a paired exercise, suggests they need all the help they can get.

Both boys are nodding as Evans and Tucker maneuver themselves. If I whipped out a measuring angle, I'm pretty confident they're nailing a ninety-degree angle on every drop step.

"Right, opposite side of the court, and the two of you try again." I hold my breath and try not to grimace as they get in position and start their slide. Tennyson is once again way too far over the invisible center line, but by some miracle, there's no collision, Maloney staying true.

Halle-fucking-lujah.

"Great job, guys." A genuine smile splits my lips, and I give two loud claps. By the time this first Collier's Creek Bisons team are high school seniors, just maybe they'll have what it takes to kick some serious ass.

A check of the clock and it's time to pack up. I've noticed the doors opening and closing a few times, meaning parents are arriving to pick up their kids. "Okay, gather around."

The fifteen boys and three girls jog on over and take a knee.

I nod in approval. This is only our second training session, and at least they've all nailed this direction. I give them the spiel about hard work and dedication. I throw in the appropriate "have fun" element before adding, "Remember, today's the deadline for volunteer coaches. If you have signed volunteer slips, place them in the box over near the door. Next week, the plan is to pick up two training sessions—one in the evening, one in the afternoon—so additional support is going to be needed."

There are several head bobs, and I just hope I get at least one volunteer who knows what they're doing. Hell, if they're not helicopter parents, that'll be a bonus.

"Training homework. Dribble and shooting those hoops, got it?"

A chorus of "Yes, Coach" fills the court, and I grin.

"Great job. Get going, then."

The kids scramble away, racing toward their parents. As I collect my clipboard, I pause, smiling when I see Maverick Evans gathering the cones and piling them in a neat stack. He's such a good kid. I angle to head in the opposite direction so we can meet in the middle. Reaching down for the bright blue cone, I startle at the deep "I'll get that, Coach."

Whipping my head in the direction of the gravelly voice, I'm met with eyes that crinkle slightly at the corners.

"Thanks." I can't stop my gaze from roaming this guy's features. Not only are his eyes an incredible blue-gray, they're also mesmerizing. Add in the way his lips are curved in a wide, friendly smile, and pulling my eyes away is a struggle.

"Will Evans, Mav's dad." He reaches out, and I take his hand eagerly. His warm grip engulfs mine.

While I might have several inches on the guy, he's more built, wider in the shoulders.

"Good to meet you, Will. Colton Green." Sure, the man knows who I am considering my training shirt states my name, but Will calling me Coach Green doesn't sit right. I reluctantly release his hand. "Mav's doing great."

"Yeah?"

"Definitely. There's some serious natural sporting talent there."

Will rubs the back of his neck, coming across as a little bashful. It's ridiculously sweet. "Thanks. He's really enjoying the training."

I bob my head, keeping eye contact rather than giving in to the desire to do a slow up and down of his body. That would be inappropriate for sure, but it's oh so tempting. "Is that all down to you? Athletic ability?" I clarify while internally reprimanding myself for my horn-dog thoughts.

Will's chuckle takes me by surprise. Not with the fact that he's laughing, but from the sweet gruffness of it that strokes against my skin and leaves goose bumps in its wake. The man is delicious personified, and try as I might, I can't shake away the flush of awareness he's sparking within me.

"The last time I shot a hoop, I realized I needed different balls to play with."

Red spreads across his cheeks so damn fast that I'm not sure whether to laugh and say, "That's what he said," or check he's okay. "I… uhm…." Will's eyes go wide, comically so, and it's no use; a loud laugh bursts free from me.

Cheeks still red, Will groans and wipes a hand across his face. Meanwhile, I know I need to get it together, but the heat in his cheeks is beyond adorable.

"I can't believe I said that."

I purse my lips and wave him off, releasing a shaky breath. "Don't mind me." I clear my throat, chasing away the last of the chuckles escaping. "A football man, huh?" I offer him an escape, which earns me a small smile. It looks good on him—a sweet smile and flushed cheeks.

Once again, he rubs at the back of his neck and gives a slightly self-deprecating shrug. "Back in the day maybe."

From the way he does a brief scan of our surroundings, it's clear that he's being modest. Well, that and he's probably looking for an escape from his mortification. Combined with the Wyoming twang I'm becoming more and more familiar with, he's quite possibly a born-and-bred local.

"You played locally, for Collier's High?"

"Nearly twenty years back, yeah."

That at least gives me a good idea of his age. "Let me guess," I say, unable to resist finding out as much about this man as possible. "Star quarterback?"

When his blush spreads quickly, I smile, finding everything about Will Evans endearing.

"Is that a yes?"

"All done, Coach." Mav's voice jolts me into awareness.

I peer down at the kid, who I now realize has the same shade of blue-gray eyes as his dad. "Good job, Evans. You got your bag?"

"Just going to grab it now, Coach." This kid is filled with so much genuine enthusiasm, he makes cleanup and collecting his stuff sound as much fun as shooting hoops. He dashes off, and I angle back to Will when he chuckles.

"*Hey, Dad. Hey, Mav. Good day?*" Amusement floods his features as he looks away from his son and meets my gaze. "Should I be offended?"

I grin at his teasing tone and his open features. "Let's take it as a win that he's having so much fun training."

He snorts. "True that." Mav calls out for his dad, and Will glances away. "That's my cue."

I bury my disappointment and bob my head, internally rolling my eyes at myself. I've had the briefest of conversations with the guy. That's it. Sure, he's fucking delectable to look at, and while I'm picking up some vibes from the man, it doesn't mean shit.

Plus, hello, inappropriate much—me panting over one of the player's dads.

"Good to meet you, Will. Have a good night." I reach out and clasp his hand, reveling in the extra eye contact the moment earns me.

"You too, Coach. Have a good night. See you next time." And then Will walks away, resting his arm across his son's shoulders as they head to the exit.

It takes me another fifteen minutes to lock up and get out of here, volunteer box under my arm. The high school grounds aren't empty, though. There's football training tonight, a sport I can respect, but it never really did it for me. The gangly frame I had while growing up motivated me to lean toward basketball, and once I'd packed on a decent amount of muscle, I spent more time than was probably healthy on a court.

I sigh at the thought and rub my hand over my

face as I get into my beat-up SUV. Between a new school, a full teaching schedule, and creating a brand-new basketball team with kids of an age I've always actively avoided, I'm tired.

Shower, food, and bed is all I have in me tonight. Sure, I may watch a show, but it can be from the comfort of my mattress. Before I pull out of the parking lot, I eye the planning sheets on the passenger seat and wonder whether I can get away with not looking over my senior chemistry classes' planning for next week's experiments.

Probably not.

Fuck. The vision of me relaxing in bed, watching reruns of *Sense8* flutters away, replaced with an image of me at the kitchen table, pen in hand, wishing it was already the weekend.

I hit the Call button on my steering wheel. "Call Cassius."

A few seconds later, the ringer sounds through the speakers. Another beat, and he picks up. "Colton. How you doing, man?"

"Remind me why I shouldn't have taken the job in Knoxville again?"

Cass's loud laughter filters through the speakers. "Because it's still in the same state as all the bullshit you left behind, and you needed as big of an escape as possible."

Somehow I manage to snort despite how gutting and true his words are. "True that." While "bullshit" seems too mild a term for all that went down, I really feel like this town can offer me the fresh start I crave.

My last two positions didn't go down great when competitive asshole parents did their "due diligence" and dragged my brother's shit out into the open.

Having a brother who is a convicted felon still serving time is always a conversation killer.

"Classes rough?"

"Ha. Hardly. Even the kids with a pain-in-the-ass rep are borderline angelic." While I was exaggerating, my last school was like a warzone in comparison. I'd take these small-town kids any day.

"So…?" He doesn't wait even a beat before he chuckles, saying, "You're not getting laid in tiny-ass-town Wyoming, huh?"

"That's not—"

"Uh-huh.

"Fuck off. You're one to talk."

"I'll have you know I've been getting plenty of action."

"Laid, Cass, *laid*. I'm not talking about how many

hours training you do every week. Not that kind of action." I roll my eyes, even though he can't see me, as I drive down the main street. There's not much open in this part of town at this time of the early evening. Mainly places to eat and a couple of bars.

"Whatever, man. I don't earn the big bucks by living for dick action."

"That right?" What he doesn't add is that he's just signed a new multimillion-dollar deal for the Minnesota Eagles, so training for him is a legit full-time job. It doesn't mean I can't wind up my long-time friend, though. "I thought you were the god of dicks."

"For fuck's sake. One comment... *one* goddamn comment about being the master of sticks or some shit, and it never leaves me."

My grin stretches wide as I signal to turn onto my street. Like most locals in town, I'm as far away from the touristy Airbnbs as possible, and I managed to pick up a steal of a quaint two-bedroom town-house. It legit takes me five minutes to drive to and from work. "If you do say stupid shit, make sure it's not in front of those basketball-playing friends of yours. They can't keep shit to themselves and gossip more than Mrs. Hendricks."

"Mrs. Hendricks?" I can imagine Cass scrunching

his forehead. "And you've got that right—about the guys, I mean."

I don't point out that Cass is probably worse than all his professional basketball player friends that I've gotten to know. We've been tight ever since I met the guy at Montview Academy when I was a senior and he a freshman, and while he'd gone on to play with the big boys and was living both our dreams, we still kept in touch.

Hell, after all that went down with my brother a few years back, he was one of the only friends I had. It's been hard lowering my guard and letting people in. Folks can be judgey fuckers. One mention of my brother serving eight years, and I see it happen, almost every time: people mulling the information over, the cagey looks sent my way.

Try as I might to not let it affect me, it does every single time. There's only so much armor I can carry before my knees buckle.

But Cassius, he's one of the best guys I know. Funny, albeit ridiculous, and honestly, despite him living a life I can't truly fathom, he's still down-to-earth.

"Were you just calling to shoot the shit or are you really regretting the move?" he asks, pulling me from my thoughts.

"Just shooting the shit, avoiding the mountain of work when I get home. You good, though? Enjoying your downtime before preseason training?"

"Yeah, all's good. Spending some time with Dylan and Mikey. Trying not to think too hard about the start of training, as there are a few new guys." I nod as he speaks, aware of the transfers and the draft addition. "Change can be a pain in the junk, but I'll just roll with it."

"You'll dominate; I have no doubt."

"Thanks, man. Shit, I've gotta go. Give me a call when you finally get laid."

"Hell fucking no. Perve. Chat soon, Cass."

"Will do. And don't forget to let me know what game you can make it out to. Tickets are yours. But hopefully I'll see you before then. See ya."

"Yeah, man. Thanks. Talk soon."

The phone cuts off just as I pull up outside my house. I take a moment to let my car idle as I stretch and crack my neck, wondering what could have been. Am I envious that Cass got his shot and made it to the big leagues? Definitely, but I'm happy for him, and every game I watch, via ESPN or in the flesh, I'm proud as hell. But this is the hand I've been dealt, and despite my bitching to Cass, I like my job, enjoy teaching. I'm even excited about the challenge of bringing basketball to Collier's Creek.

But getting laid, though…. Yeah, that would be nice.

I switch off the engine and grab the planning sheets, volunteer box, laptop, and training gear. A few steps later, I'm entering my dark house—miraculously without dropping anything—and flicking on the lights.

Nice. I shake my head at using such a lame descriptor for hooking up, but it's been a long-ass time, and I would settle for a mediocre lay at this point.

I've leaned into a bit of gossip in school, so I know I'm not the only gay guy in town. Pretty sure there's other men and women from the community around, too, but settling in has taken all my focus. Plus being a teacher in a small town comes with its own set of issues. Me fucking my way around would cause a stir, which means I expect it's going to be me and my right hand for the foreseeable future.

An image of Will pops into my head, and I smirk. At least meeting the stormy-gray-eyed sexy-as-fuck man has given me fresh spank bank material.

CHAPTER TWO

WILL

THERE ARE TWO THINGS IN LIFE YOU CAN GUARANTEE I'll do. One is doing whatever I can to make my kid happy. The second is cleaning up a mess, even if I'm not the one to cause it. It's a compulsion and a little frustrating at times, but it is what it is.

Making my kid happy today means tugging on a pair of sweatpants that I realize are ten years old and suitable for the ass I had when I was nine pounds lighter. But they fit, just. I'm not exactly sure they're suitable to be seen wearing in public, though.

But Mav dragging me out of the house thirty minutes before his basketball training, as apparently basketball is life, means I've got no choice but to roll with it.

I can only hope the extra baggy T-shirt I pulled

out of my closet covers my ass and groin enough to not have any kids crying or parents calling the sheriff on me.

Fuck. Wide-eyed, I lift my hand and give a wave of acknowledgement to Sheriff Morgan. He offers me an up-nod just as he gets in his patrol car. Jesus. How about that for conjuring! All I need now is for him to pull me over and write me up for indecent exposure.

"You know we don't have to be early every session, right?" I dart a quick glance into the rearview as I speak, briefly catching Mav's eyes. Am I a little reluctant considering the epic humiliation of my "balls" comment last week? Possibly. Apparently, if I'm going to make a dick of myself, I go all in.

"But you're one of the assistant coaches now, Dad. It makes you official and stuff. Plus you'll need to speak to Coach about what you need to do."

My lips twitch at his enthusiasm, and it's likely the only thing stopping me from panicking about Mav talking me into volunteering to help with training sessions. And the fact that Coach Green accepted.

A flash of movement out the window draws my attention to Logan. My smile comes easily as I give him a friendly wave. He's locking up the bookstore, a place Mav loves. It reminds me, we need to get an order in for the latest Derek Landy book. There's nothing like a shared appreciation of sarcasm to bring me and my son together.

Since Mav has never shown the slightest interest in sports before, despite my efforts, when he latched on to the new basketball team in town, I didn't hesitate to offer my support. Anything to get him active, away from his Xbox, and grinning. But I have no real idea what to expect. Hell, I don't know if Coach Green has been overwhelmed with volunteers and has selected me from the multitude or he's been scrambling for any help, and I'm the only sucker who's signed up.

Either way, I'm in it now, but I still have no idea how involved he wants me to be or even what he expects.

I wasn't exaggerating when I had a conversation with him last week. Basketball is not my game. I've probably watched a handful of games in my life, and I use the term "watch" loosely. But for Mav, I'll try.

"Just make sure you treat me like everyone else, okay, Dad? No babying or embarrassing me." Mav shoots a quirked eyebrow my way, looking so much like his mom that my heart aches a little.

"Embarrassing? Me?" I tut as I pull into the parking lot. "I'm, like, the coolest of cool and am… *like*… down with the kids."

An overexaggerated sigh spills from Mav. "*Dad….*" It's an honest-to-god whine. I swallow down my laughter, not-so-secretly loving getting a rise out of my son. "And that right there, saying you're 'down' and 'cool,' is exactly the sort of thing you shouldn't be saying outside of this car, 'kay?"

"So I can say it, *like*"—I emphasize the word like the good dad I am—"all the time in the car and with you? How about with the windows open, *like*? I could yell it out—"

"And it's time to leave." Mav pushes open the car door like his ass is on fire, and I grin, following him while calling out to remind him to look out for cars.

When we step into the high school gym, the lights are on, some equipment is out, but there's no one in sight. We're still twenty-five minutes early, but I'm surprised there aren't other early birds. While my hometown is small and a lot more relaxed than the hustle of Boston, where I settled after college and started my business, anything new to the town usually comes with an air of excitement. And basketball is most definitely new.

Movement to my right grabs my attention.

Coach Green appears out of the storeroom, a bag of basketballs in his grip.

"Hey," I call out and head in his direction. "Put me and Mav to work, Coach."

"Will, hey." A wide smile is directed my way. Coach Green was open and friendly when we met last week, and then again when he emailed me about supporting the new team. And that he didn't ride me for the awkward innuendo must mean he's a half-decent guy.

Though, just the thought of "ride" and "Coach Green" in the same sentence makes my brain stutter. But this is so not the time.

Bad Will.

A bubble of anticipation forms in my gut as I shake his hand. I could do with a new friend, one without history in Collier's Creek. And a person who doesn't immediately look at me with sadness, like I'm wounded, and offer condolences; I could definitely do with a friend like that.

"Thanks for coming in early." He glances at Mav, who's all but vibrating with anticipation. "You ready for some hard work on the court today, Mav?"

"Absolutely, Coach. I've been practicing my drills, and Grandpa helped Dad put up a hoop on the garage over the weekend."

"Yeah?" Coach Green darts his attention to me, a sparkle in his eyes, his smile still big and friendly. "Sounds like your grandpa and dad are looking out for you. You want to go grab those cones and split the court into three for me?"

"Sure thing, Coach." Mav runs off, his eagerness making my heart happy.

"Sounds like you had a busy weekend." He puts the bag down and indicates for me to follow him.

I move to his side, and we walk over to a few benches where I spot some paperwork spread out across the bench, saying, "Not *that* busy. My dad's handy with a power tool. Me, not so much, Coach."

"Colton," he says, casting a quick glance my way. "Well, when the kids aren't around."

"Colton." I nod. "Got it." I don't have the chance to say anything else before he picks up the clipboard, and it looks like we're getting down to business. I just hope I don't make a dick of myself too spectacularly when he realizes my lack of knowledge is real and I wasn't being modest.

"So, we're going to do a few basic drills. I want you focusing on defense."

"O-kay…."

Colton passes me a stack of papers complete with

dot points and illustrations. I exhale in relief. Since he starts to chuckle, I'm assuming he saw.

"Don't worry, Will. I wouldn't throw you in the deep end." He tilts his head at me, his lips twitching, which he's already done more than once in the two times we've met. "Well, I would, but not without pretty diagrams." His laugh is deep and infectious. My gaze drops to his mouth, completely caught up in the sound. "So…" He clears his throat, and I snap my attention up, making eye contact, hating the flush that I feel spreading across my cheeks. Again.

Fucking hell. Colton is going to think I'm a dork or a dick. Probably both.

The worst thing?

I have no idea why I'm a bumbling idiot around the guy.

"The defense plays."

"Right, yes, defense." I nod as though I have a clue what he's talking about. It's likely his lips are twitching again, but I refuse to check.

"If you can work with a small group and focus on the first three drills on your list, we'll get a game going on after that."

At his expectant look, I quickly bob my head. "Yeah, sure. So just run them through these?" I glance at the sheet. I've got this. Sure, it's not football, but it's a sport, and the kids are under twelve, so it means I'll figure it out. Right?

"That's right. All the kids have done these drills before. Just make sure they're focused, and if they mess up or slack off, pull them up."

Okay, that makes me feel a little better. Wrangling kids, I can manage. In my former life before returning to my childhood town, I ran my own company right alongside my business partner. Overseeing so many staff and constantly putting out fires while battling coding means I've grown skilled at navigating chaos.

A bunch of energized kids, I can handle.

"Who else is helping out?" I ask, turning my focus back to Colton.

A wince and two lines form between his brows. "Uhm… we're it."

"We are?" He bobs his head, and I cringe a little inside, saying, "Well, hell. I'll apologize in advance that you're stuck with me." The poor guy really has scraped the bottom of the barrel having to rely on me.

A warm chuckle escapes him. "I'm sure we'll make a great team."

Not going to lie, I bask in his confidence, warmth filling my chest. I'm pretty sure pink is slowly creeping into my cheeks too. "I'll make sure I watch a few League games so I'm not completely clueless. Do some reading up."

I see the moment it registers that I'm not teasing. His brows shoot high. "You've never watched any basketball?"

"Well…." I clear my throat, my neck and face heating. "My college roommate enjoyed the game, so it was regularly on in the background. When he'd cheer, I'd look up occasionally to see what all the fuss is about."

He parts his lips, but rather than speaking, he huffs out a laugh. "Okay. Well, this is something we can remedy. Perhaps over the weekend we can watch one of last season's games together, and I can talk you through it." He turns his head, and I see him seek out Mav before turning his attention back to me. But rather than making eye contact, his gaze lowers. I have a moment of panic remembering my tight-as-fuck sweatpants, then I realize where his focus is traveling.

My left hand.

I clench my hand into a fist on instinct. I fucking hate this part and have no idea if my reaction will ever be different.

Before he can say anything, I rush out with "I can

drop Mav off at my parents'. They're desperate for any time they can get with him. I think Dad's even put a hoop up at their place." Colton makes eye contact. "Just let me know when and where. I don't want to make a complete shambles of this and have to turn in my best dad award," I say, forcing myself to relax and trying to ease into a joke to cut through the unasked questions I can see in his eyes, "so watching a game would be great."

"Excellent."

I exhale when he doesn't push.

"I'll text you the details." His smile is back. "Right, well, I figure we're going to start getting the rest of the players here in the next five minutes, so why don't I talk you through those drills while we get the chance?"

My nod is quick as I hold out the papers so we can both see the details. Maybe this coaching gig will work out, and hanging out over the weekend, perhaps even with a beer…. Yeah, that definitely sounds like something I need in my life.

CHAPTER THREE

COLTON

Is it bad that I live for the weekends? Don't get me wrong, I love teaching. Love seeing that lightbulb moment when my students finally understand the material. It's rewarding, and even when I'm buried in grading and planning, it's the reason I keep going.

But it's finally Saturday, and for once, I have no homework or assessments to fill up my weekend. With just a bit of planning to do tomorrow, I can kick back this Saturday.

That means grabbing a coffee from CC's before going to the store for groceries, and then I get to hang out with Will. A shiver of anticipation shoots up my spine at the thought.

The man is *fine*. Hello, did you see those sweat-pants during practice? I all but swallowed my tongue when I gobbled up the sight of him. But he's clearly so much more than a sexy guy in sinful gray sweats. In fact, I'm pretty sure he needs a friend. It was there in the way his eyes lit up at the invite for him to stop by and watch a game. While he doesn't exactly scream lonely, there's something about him, about his sweet shyness and the way his cheeks heat that makes me think he doesn't have many friends.

Which is weird, right? Not that I'm one to talk considering my own social life, or rather lack of it.

I've learned enough to know that Will's parents are involved in his and Mav's lives. He's also a Collier's Creek local who went to the very same high school I now teach at. This town is small enough and my workplace gossipy enough that while there's a hub of small towns within a fifty-mile radius that feed into the high school, it's a community with strong history and multiple generations of residents.

But maybe I've got it wrong. Perhaps I'm reading into his eagerness to spend time with me because I'm the one who's new and haven't quite found my feet yet.

Either way, I'm looking forward to getting to know the guy, and despite what he said about the lack of basketball knowledge, he had no issues handling the two training sessions last week. I may have got wrapped up in staring at him once or twice.

The scent of fresh coffee greets me, the aroma filtering through the open door of CC's. This place has become my local haunt on Saturdays. Not only does it make for a pleasant walk from my house through town to get here—taking roughly twenty minutes—the coffee is divine. Surprised the heck out of me too. My experience of small-town coffee hasn't been particularly pleasant. Hell, a few places I've dropped into over the years have only just rivalled instant crap I have little choice but to gulp down in the staffroom.

My smile is instant when I step inside, but rather than spotting the manager, Cameron, my gaze lands on Will. He's laughing at something a customer is saying while he's at the huge, shiny machine, making coffees.

He works here?

In all the times I've visited the place, not once have I seen Will out and about, and definitely not here. I would have noticed. There's no way a man like Will can blend into the background.

I get into line, my gaze not wavering from Will and the way he's smiling, bobbing his head at something the woman before me is saying to him.

"…none of that, Will." She tuts, but her amusement is obvious. "I need all the syrupy sweetness. It's the only thing that helps me put up with Hank and constantly having to scrub the oil stains he leaves on everything he touches."

"I don't believe that for a minute, Francine." Will winks at her, and I'm sure I hear her sigh a little. *I get it, Francine. I really do.* "Here you go." He leans over and passes Francine her drink. "Complete with all the vanilla syrup even though you don't need the added sweetness."

As Francine reaches for her drink, Will's gaze travels my way. His eyebrows lift, a fresh, warm smile forming on his lips. At the movement and his "Hey," Francine turns my way, eyeing me up and down.

"You're the new science teacher." Interests fills her gaze.

I'm not even surprised by this sort of observation from the locals. It's something I've learned to roll with. "Yes, ma'am." I nod. "Colton Green."

She bobs her head and then peers back at Will, who's moved from the coffee machine to the serving counter. "I'll be off, Will. You give that kid of yours a hug from me."

"Will do, Francine."

She turns back to me, scrutinizes me for a beat, apparently mulling over before she walks away.

Amused, I press my lips together and step up to the counter. "Hey. I didn't know you worked here." Will being a barista boggles my mind a little. I have the utmost respect for anyone who feeds my caffeine addiction, but I never figured it's what Will did for a living. Maybe it's the new Jeep Cherokee that I spotted him driving last week, which I know makes me sound judgey as hell. But damn, I drive a rust bucket.

He can't make that much in tips, right?

His smile is warm and immediately sends awareness prickling over my body. "For a few years now."

Surprise shoots my brows high again. "Really?" I shake my head. "Funny that I've never seen you here before."

"That'll be because I don't usually work weekends and only tend to work school hours. I'm just covering Cameron for a couple of hours, which wasn't a problem as Mav stayed with my parents last night."

"So, home alone?" I'm totally fishing. Last week when we'd arranged our game watching, a weird vibe had come from him when I checked out his left hand. Just because he said his parents would take care of Mav and he doesn't wear a ring doesn't mean there's not someone waiting for him at home.

"Yeah. Rare these days, but no lazy day." He finishes with a light chuckle, and since I spot restless movement out the corner of my eye, I figure I need to order so he can get on with his job. "So, what'll it be?"

"A large cappuccino would be great. Perhaps add one of those blueberry muffins too."

He rings up my order and asks, "You want this to go or…?"

It's what I usually do, but I spy a free seat at the high-top table that just happens to be near the counter. It's where I'll be heading. "I'll grab that table there."

"I'll bring it over." He passes me my plated muffin.

"Thanks."

It doesn't take long for Will to appear at my side, pulling me away from checking my emails. He puts my mug down and smiles. "Mind if I join you?"

"Yeah, sure. Of course," I stumble. "You're finished?" When he indicates over his shoulder, I see Cameron.

Will sits opposite me at the small high-top. "He got back a little earlier than I expected."

I bob my head and pick up my coffee, taking a tentative sip in case it scorches my mouth. I sigh into the taste, my shoulders relaxing.

"Do you actually want to be alone?"

I flick my eyes up, making eye contact, but don't miss the smirk or the quirked eyebrow. I put down my mug, a grin splitting my mouth. "What can I say? I like my coffee." I point at the mug. "And that there is a pretty spectacular cup."

Another small blush touches his cheeks. "Good to know the part-time jobs I had when I was in college didn't go to waste." His chuckle is a little self-deprecating, but I grab on to the extra information he shared about going to school.

"Definitely not. Best not tell Cameron, but honestly, the best cappuccino I've had since moving here."

"Your secret's safe with me. Where'd you move from?"

"I was out in Jackson, Tennessee, for three years, and before that I was in Kentucky."

His eyebrows shoot high. "You're a long way from home."

Exactly the way I want it to be. "Yeah. I was ready for a change." *And an escape from my nightmare family.*

"This job came up, plus it included a relocation package. It was hard to say no to."

It helped that once I disclosed my history and the facts about my brother's incarceration, the principal had barely blinked, simply thanking me for my honesty and letting me know I'd be a welcome addition to his school.

After taking a sip of his coffee, Will bobs his head. "I can appreciate the need for change, and the school's lucky to have you."

His compliment makes my stomach bubble. "Well, I'm not sure my senior chemistry class would agree with you." A teasing smile forms on my lips.

"Chemistry?" He blows out a low whistle. "The hard subjects, huh?"

"The fun and challenging," I shoot back before adding, "And the subject where I pray daily no one's going to blow the lab up." I laugh, easing into the banter. "And how about you? Did you move straight back to town after college?"

"I spent about fifteen years in Boston."

I bob my head, intrigued about what brought him back. Sure, he has a son, but given Mav's age, he didn't move straight back to have a family, unless I'm way off with his age. Rather than fishing for more information, I stick to safer topics, the memory of last week's reaction heavy in my mind.

"Mav seems really at home, settled." Sure, I've only met the boy a few times, but he's confident and a good kid.

When Will's face lights up, I know my topic choice was the right move. "He loves it here, close to his grandparents. They spoil him rotten. Being in a small town isn't so bad."

"Oh, William, there you are."

My brows shoot up while Will smiles at an older lady who interrupts us.

"Geraldine." Will sends me an apologetic look before returning his gaze to her. "What can I help you with?"

"You're not working." Narrowed eyes point Will's way, and my lips twitch at the accusation in her tone.

"That's correct. I don't work weekends."

Somehow, her eyes narrow even closer together, which is pretty impressive. "But Francine said you served her."

A light chuckle falls from his lips. His laugh is nice, sexy, even when trying to fend off this older lady, who apparently has an opinion about Will being here. "That's right. I was just filling in for Cameron, but he's back now."

"Hmm… but Barkasaurus Rex likes the way you make his special doggy foam treat the best."

Barkasaurus Rex? It's tempting to interrupt—I have so many questions—but I think better of it.

"Thank you. That's high praise," he says without even the slightest hint of a smile. "But Cameron is the master of the dog foam treats. Honestly, he taught me how to make it. He'll look after you and Barky."

She doesn't look convinced, and for the first time, she glances my way. Her head tilts as her gaze roams over me. I offer her a smile, not quite sure what to expect from her.

"You're the new teacher."

"I am. Colton Green," I introduce.

She sniffs, still staring at me. "I've heard about you."

My stomach drops. *Not again. Not so soon.* I keep my smile fixed in place. "All good things, I hope."

"Well, yes."

I barely hold back my heavy breath of relief. With the way Will's still sporting an amused expression, I think I'm in the clear. "That's wonderful. No doubt when testing time comes, that will change."

"Hmm. Well, if you see me in the street and I have my Barky with me, be sure to come and admire him. He's a beautiful Bichon Frise."

"Yes, of course." It's not like I can say anything else.

"Good." She turns back to Will. "I'll go and ask Cameron if he can make a foamy treat as good as you." Her sigh is heavy as she spins around and leaves us.

"O-kay…," I say pointedly to Will. "A friend of yours?"

This time, Will's chuckle is loud. I like it even better, especially the way his eyes crease. "That's Geraldine."

"And Barkasaurus Rex?"

He snorts, the sound so abrupt, it tears a laugh from me. "Barkasaurus Rex is a mutt. Ugly thing, but harmless."

"So not a Bichon Frise?"

A wide smile forms. "Not the last time I looked." He shakes his head. "Sorry about that. I *was* saying being in a small town isn't so bad." A cute wince follows.

"And you want to amend that statement?" I jest.

"It has its charms."

I snicker at his word choice. Though, he is right.

Collier's Creek has a certain quirky charm to it. "It's going to be an adjustment, I think."

Will chuckles. "I can see that. Does that mean you've also been subjected to the joy of the knitting group and the old farmers' crew?"

"I'm kind of nervous to say no, but it sounds like I have lots to look forward to." I take another mouthful of my drink, thinking about the interesting characters I've spotted in the street.

"Perhaps avoid said circus for a while longer if you can."

"They that bad?"

His grin stretches wide. "Not bad, per se. More like nosey and getting involved in your business given half a chance."

"I'll be sure to keep on the lookout."

He snickers again, the sound rich and warm. This time when his eyes crinkle at the sides, I can't stop myself from wanting to know, well, everything about him.

Is he single? Where's Mav's mom? Is he straight?

All the things I'll hopefully discover in time. At least I hope so, as I want to know more. So now seems like the perfect time to start.

"So, now that you're free, what are your plans?"

Sure, we're meeting up later, but that's about seven or so hours from now.

"Other than basketball 101 with you, if that's still on, nothing at all."

I'm nodding before he's finished. "Absolutely. I was thinking of heading to the school gym for an hour, but if perhaps you want to play some one-on-one instead… it'd be a good precursor to tonight's game." I push a hint of teasing into my tone, eager to spend some more time with the man.

While I hadn't planned on working out at the gym until tomorrow, I'm more than happy to play all the cards I have.

"Yeah, sure," he says eagerly, a glimmer of amusement in his gaze as he adds, "But seriously, go easy on me. Everything I've said about my inexperience wasn't an exaggeration."

The sordid and absolutely wishfully thinking mind of mine can't help but wonder if he's only talking about basketball.

"Shit." My hands snap out, and I grab onto Will's shoulders, exhaling when I manage to save him. He already has scuffed knees, a bleeding elbow, and I'm pretty sure I have a bruise forming on my ass.

"I'm sorry," he all but whispers, the warmth of his breath brushing me as we remain close. "Are you about to give up on me?"

There's a playful rush to his words that my body tries to respond to. Swallowing down the heady lust his closeness creates, I focus on grinning and reluctantly release him and step away. "Nah. It was either you or Mr. Ellis from Ellis Books. I think your role is safe."

He snorts a laugh. "So you are stuck with me, huh? Maybe I just need to give you a big blanket apology for that." He steps fully away and goes in search of the ball that he dropped when he all but body-slammed me.

For an athletic guy, one who spent years on the football field, he absolutely doesn't have any real skill on the court. Though, he's so much of a distraction, I'm not convinced he couldn't win a one-on-one game against me.

"I think this is my cue to admit defeat." He rubs his free hand over his hazelnut-brown hair, the longer strands shifting and falling lightly back into place.

I follow the movement, unable to resist eating

him up. "Perhaps lick your wounds with chicken wings at Jake's Tap?"

"Chicken wings I can do." A bright smile follows his words. "I may need to go and clean up first."

The small grazes dotting his body need some TLC, and I have half a mind to offer my services.

"Perhaps we can meet there after freshening up? You're not the only one who could do with a hose down."

At my words, Will's gaze rakes over my sweat-soaked T-shirt. It's a slow drag that heats me up, prickling my skin with awareness. His gaze snaps to mine, and he jerks his attention away and back again as pink floods his cheeks. Wide-eyed, he stares at me.

Interesting.

"Right, thirty minutes all good?" I say quickly, an easy smile on my face.

While I have no idea what Will is thinking, his surprise is obvious. I'm just not sure if he's uncomfortable or embarrassed. Hell, maybe he's neither or both.

Either way, I want to make him comfortable. Call me selfish, but the little I've spent with the man, I've enjoyed. And I want more.

CHAPTER FOUR

WILL

Maybe it was the sweat and the way it made his tee cling to his broad shoulders. Maybe it was simply the way he focused on me with such sweet, open intensity that got under my skin. Whatever it was that made my brain short-circuit, a cool shower and the sting from cleaning my knees haven't done a thing to dull my interest.

And isn't that a hell of a thing?!

That my reaction is for a man isn't the surprise. Sure, the last time I was with a guy was in college, but that isn't what's throwing me for the loop. The truth is, I wish that was the issue. Instead, the feelings that keep bubbling in my gut, threatening to get my dick hard and my breath catching, have guilt edging my conscience.

Rationally, I know it's okay… the racing of my pulse, the way my gaze drifts to Colton's lips when he laughs, smiles, says something that makes me grin. But five years of mourning my wife, years of focusing on taking each hour, day, week, and month at a time while making sure I'm everything to Mav is difficult to process.

Colton's just finished telling me about an overzealous parent from a school he used to work at, and I'm hanging on to every word he's saying.

"It took five cops to restrain them and get them under control."

A laugh bursts from me, and I shake my head, equally amused and full of disbelief. "They seriously started a brawl on the court?"

"Well, less of a brawl, more of a pile up as they argued over the ball."

"And suddenly I don't feel so bad about not pushing Mav into sports."

His chuckle ripples over me, a happy caress. "Helicopter and competitive sports parents are in a league of their own. And from the looks of it, I'd say you're doing an incredible job with Mav."

The compliment washes over me, and not for the first time, heat floods my cheeks. "He's a good kid," I deflect and pick up my bottle, finishing off the last gulp of beer.

Rather than challenge me, which I'm super grateful for, Colton instead eyes my empty bottle. "Two's my limit for driving," he says.

I bob my head in agreement. I deliberately chose a light beer, since I drove to Jake's Tap, but they went down super easy.

"You want to head back to mine now? Start your coaching education?" The teasing tone clear in his voice has me grinning and my embarrassment at his compliment easing.

"Sounds good." I stand, peering over at the bar. Once I catch Jodi's eye, I raise my hand in farewell, not wanting to interrupt the conversation she's having with Logan.

As we head to the exit, Nash Vigil crosses my path. "Oh, hey, Nash." I reach out and shake my old school friend's rough hand.

His eyes brighten as he greets me. "Good to see you, Will. I haven't seen you outside the four walls of CC's for a while."

I chuckle. "Collier's residents and their caffeine addiction keep me kind of busy."

He bobs his head, aiming a small smile my way.

When he cuts his attention to Colton, I remember myself. "Have you met Colton Green yet?"

"I can't say I have."

They shake hands. As they do, my gaze travels to Colton's exposed forearm. The strip of muscles, the splattering of soft hair covered by what I can only imagine is soft skin looks all kinds of delectable. How the hell did I not realize how sexy forearms could be?

"You're the guy who's bringing basketball to town, huh?" There's a twinkle in Nash's eyes, reminding me what a good guy he is and that I should really try to catch up with him properly. He's probably just eaten too. Even back at school, Nash was known for getting super hangry.

"For my sins," Colton answers. Fuck, he's handsome when he wears a sweet, coy smile. "I teach at the high school but managed to get wrangled into starting a basketball team. We're having a ton of fun, though."

Nash bobs his head, his gaze darting between the two of us. "Is Mav in the team?"

"He is. He dreams, lives, and talks nonstop about basketball these days."

"I'd say that's a pretty good review of your new team," he directs at Colton. Angling back to me, he says, "You should bring Mav over to Twisted Pine Ranch sometime. Let him have a ride."

Colton shifts a little at my side, his arm brushing against mine. Awareness shoots goose bumps over my skin. "Yeah." I clear my throat. "I'm sure Mav would love that. Thanks, Nash." I reach out once more to shake his hand, letting him know we're going to head out.

"Just let me know." Nash focuses once again on Colton, his intense gaze studying the man at my side. "Feel free to join Will and Mav when they come out."

There's a subtle shift in Colton's body, a loss of tension. "Yeah," he says brightly. "That sounds great, thanks. It's been a while since I've ridden, but it could be fun." He peers at me, an unspoken question in his gaze.

The awareness is back. The zip of... *something* that threatens to catch my breath. "Definitely. We'll make it happen."

After saying goodbye, I'm stopped three times on our way out. Once by Kyle asking about my parents, then by Hank who wants to know if he can expect the pumpkin spice back in the coffee shop anytime soon. After one more minor interrogation, I exhale when the sweet fresh air hits me.

"Hell…." Colton's wide-eyed and amused. "It's like hanging out with another celebrity." He peers over at me as we head toward the small parking lot. "It usually like that?"

I roll my eyes and shake my head. "I really wish I could say no."

"But you'd be lying?"

I side-eye him and bob my head. "That…. So much that." I angle toward my car and pause when we reach the hood. "And don't think I missed your 'another celebrity' comment." I quirk my brow, an easy grin pulling at my lips as I back up and lean against my Jeep. "You spend a lot of time hanging out with famous people?"

Colton is standing directly in front of me. Not quite so close that I can feel his breath against my skin, but he's in grabbing distance and in my space enough that I have to tilt my head a little to make eye contact. His deep-brown eyes are full of humor, but it's the way the tip of his tongue peeks out, dampening his bottom lip, that has my heart racing.

"Athletes more than celebrities. But," he continues, angling his head a little to the side, "I could just as well give you the name of the man who invented basketball, since the likelihood of you having heard of any of the athletes are slim to none."

My grin is instant and positively wicked as I take great delight in saying, "What, James Naismith? A famous basketball player"—I quirk my eyebrow, thoroughly pleased with myself—"has the same name as the inventor? That's lucky. Would have been awkward if they'd been called Walter Camp." I bounce my brows for good measure.

A startled laugh escapes him. "How the fuck do you know Naismith invented basketball?"

I give a careless shrug.

"Well, aren't you just full of surprises."

My heart stutters before booming loudly against my rib cage. Colton's flirting with me. Sure, I'm out of practice and have usually already put a mile between me and anyone who's shown the slightest interest, but fuck if I don't like his attention.

"I'm more than an excellent barista." The tease, the flirtatious tone feels alien, but I don't shy away from it.

"Of that I have little doubt."

When did he get so close? Feeling nothing but air behind me means I'm apparently the one who moved away from my SUV. The sound of an engine startles me, and I jerk my attention in that direction. It's enough to clear my head and cut through the invisible strings tugging us together.

"You want to follow me?" he asks.

I search his gaze. Did I just imagine a moment?

Nothing about Colton screams fazed or affected. Hell, maybe I ordered the wrong beer and I'm not as sober as I thought. I take stock and immediately disregard that. There's no buzz of alcohol in my system.

"You okay?"

Shit. "Yeah, sorry, following you would be great. Thanks." I've barely finished speaking before I'm easing open my door.

Escape and hide it is.

My floundering is messing with my head. Perhaps I should just go home.

The thought of leaving settles like lead in my stomach. And that right there is my answer. I've always listened to and followed my gut. Or at least tried to.

It brought me back home. It took me to the meeting where I first met my wife, Kelly. Just maybe it led me here because it's exactly where I'm meant to be.

There's only one way to find out.

THE SOUND SPILLING OUT OF ME WOULD EMBARRASS the hell out of me if I were sober. But after too many beers to count, I simply laugh harder.

"The fuck was that sound?" Colton barely gets out the words, he's laughing so hard.

I can't answer. Can't speak. Too lost in my snorting laughter. Waving a hand in front of my face is all I can manage.

"Seriously…. Not sure if it's a howler monkey impersonation or—"

"Fuck off," I manage with zero heat, my cheeks hurting from spending most of our day and night grinning and snickering. "It's your damn fault."

There's not a single drop of remorse in his vibrant eyes. Sure, my vision is a happy level of hazy, but I don't see double of Colton.

Fuck…. Two Coltons? With just the one of him, I'm feeling consumed. Two and I'd be lost forever.

"Me?"

I'm not buying his innocent tone. The shine in his gaze is too bright, too self-satisfied for that.

"Yes you, Mr. Let's Play Beer Pong Despite Being Practically Twenty Years Out of College."

He quirks one of his eyebrows and sways a little. "I wasn't the one who started raising the stakes."

It's true. And despite my shit talk, I'm not even

sorry. How can I be when each time he laughs, the sound caresses my skin, reminding me what it's like to lose myself in the moment.

To laugh. To let loose.

And—I'm sure to god—flirt.

It's addictive, this feeling, how Colton makes me remember.

And raising the stakes?

Well, we started with shots, progressed to a ridiculous, playful game of truth or dare, which led to an incident involving shaving foam…. Okay, apparently we're reliving our frat days. And I don't mind one bit.

I've finally managed to get myself under control enough to take a deep breath without snickering. I can feel by the twitch of my lips, though, that I'm just on the edge. It won't take much to break down into snorting laughter again.

The snap into hysteria has brought a natural conclusion to the game. We gravitate to Colton's kitchen. We've already eaten burgers and so many potato chips, I'm going to be regretting them tomorrow.

"Sweet or savory?" Colton's at the fridge, peering inside. It's when he leans over, his juicy ass sticking out just so, that my brain gets fried.

He mentioned an ex-boyfriend from a few years back, so I know he's not straight. He's also single, and fuck if the best night I've had in years doesn't get my junk twitching at the thought of making it even better.

Colton glancing back at me over his shoulder has my attention snapping up. Heat pours into my cheeks, and from the tilt of his head, the question in his gaze, I'm sure he caught me staring.

"Sweet or savory?" he repeats. There's a gruffness in his voice that wasn't there the first time he asked.

"Both?" The word slips out, the inflection high, not quite strangled, as I'm a thirty-nine-year-old man, fuck you very much. I'm simply choosing to ignore the flash of awareness I'm feeling and how I'm struggling to keep my mind out of the gutter.

"Both it is." Colton's eye contact keeps me hostage another beat until he finally turns his attention to the refrigerator.

From the heat rushing through me, I have half a mind to take over rustling through the fridge just so I can cool down. It has nothing to do with liking the idea of being pressed up against him.

Knowing I'm standing here like an awkward dufus, I exhale and roll my eyes at myself, finally finding my voice. "Do you need me to get plates?"

Keeping my hands busy will stop me from getting into trouble and potentially wrecking a good night.

I can't help but keep going back and forth on whether to act on my desire.

Will it ruin the night or improve it?

Am I starting to overthink things? For sure. There's no point even making up excuses for myself. Not when I know exactly why I'm starting to feel uncomfortable.

Colton's response of "Yeah, the cupboard to the left of the stove" pulls me out of my spiral.

"No problem." I get moving while he starts pulling cheeses and salami out of his refrigerator. It gives me the chance to crack my neck and organize the plates before I down a glass of water.

Amusement colors his words. "Thirsty?" But when I look at him, concern blazes in his gaze.

I stop drinking and quickly catch the drip that wants to trickle down my chin. Colton tracks the movement, his gaze intense enough to make me catch my breath.

"I really want to kiss you."

Surprise floods his features at my words, his gaze snapping to mine, and I'm sure as fuck just as spun out as he is.

"Uhm… shit." An awkward low laugh spills from me. "Sorry, I didn't mean to say that."

Wide-eyed, Colton continues to stare at me. Talk about screwing things up and ruining our great day.

It's time to retreat. To leave before—

"You don't want to kiss me, or you didn't mean to tell me?"

The room is still as I stand frozen, my planned retreat disintegrating under the weight of his gaze. He's waiting for me to answer, and I will. I just wish the adrenaline of the past few minutes hadn't sobered me up.

"It's not the kind of thing I usually just let slip." Feeling self-conscious, I run a hand through my hair and release a halfhearted chuckle. When he doesn't budge, doesn't respond, I relent, saying, "But yeah, I want to kiss you." My breathing picks up, despite trying to calm the hell down.

When the fuck did all this become so hard?

Being out of my depth is no fun, but from the goose bumps spreading across my skin and the flutter of wings in my stomach, I can't deny the excitement.

His smile is slow, sinfully decadent as it lifts his lips. The quirk of his eyebrow is a challenge.

It's up to me to take it.

Step up and follow through.

Since I started this whole thing, I need to make it happen.

With steady steps that are the complete opposite to how quickly I want to rush him, I make my way toward Colton. Soulful eyes watch my approach, expectation front and center—inviting and full of promise.

Nerves bounce around my chest. Fear, wonder, and a hint of desperation have me reaching for Colton's waist as soon as I'm before him.

"Hey," I whisper, my voice unsteady. Do I feel like a dick for my choice of word? Definitely. But this is a big deal. Maybe not for Colton, a hot guy who's funny and sexy, and I have little doubt he hooks up whenever he wants.

But me?

"Hey."

I grin at him a little sheepishly, but I'm grateful for how he responded.

Despite the material of his T-shirt separating my hand from his skin, warmth presses against my palm. Another fizz of excitement bubbles to life. I feel like a clueless virgin, filled with uncertainty and the likelihood of premature ejaculation.

I want this. Want his lips on mine. Want to

remember how another person tastes. Learn how to feel again. And fuck if I don't want to shoot my load with someone's hand or lips around my cock.

"Are you o—"

I capture his words, press my lips to his, no longer able to hold back.

Opening my mouth, I slide my tongue along his lip, thrilling at his low growl and the way he hooks his arm around me.

I'm practically on my tiptoes, leaning up, trying to get as close to him as possible while our mouths collide, turning hot, needy, the pressure so perfect, I happily get lost in the moment.

Needing his body pressed against mine, I wrap my arm around his back, drawing him in, deepening the kiss, enjoying the tingling in my lips and the hard planes of his body against mine. When he palms my butt cheek, a fresh shudder of desire trickles through me. His warm hand is unfamiliar, strong, and feels so delicious, I'm not even embarrassed by the groan spilling from my lips.

He smiles against my mouth and angles back, capturing my gaze. "You want to move this to the couch?"

The bed…, I'm tempted to answer. My hard cock begs me to, but it's too much, too soon. Instead, I nod, not willing to stop kissing him just yet. Well, only if for a moment so we can get more comfortable.

He presses a light kiss against my lips, and I sigh into it, reluctantly letting him go when he steps away.

His gaze moves to the food covering the bench. "You still hungry?"

"Yeah, but I'll pass on the food." Feeling brave, knowing he wants to get back to making out as keenly as I do, my grin comes easily.

He groans and tilts his head back, his eyes closing as he directs his face to the ceiling. "Fuck!" He shakes his head, his gaze snapping to mine. "You're so fucking sexy."

Heat slams into me. It's been a beat since I've been hit on, let alone been called sexy. With my focus solely on Mav since losing Kelly, I haven't given myself time to even consider the possibility.

I wait for the guilt to hit me.

Nothing.

Wait for the freak-out to start.

When it doesn't, a smile splits my face, and I don't give Colton time to react beyond following me as I reach for his hand and drag him out of the kitchen.

CHAPTER FIVE

COLTON

WE HIT MY LARGE COUCH IN A TANGLE OF LIMBS. I scramble for his buttons, desperate to get my hands on his warm skin. When I finally tear off his shirt and he mine, we cling to each other, barely parting for breath as we kiss the ever-loving shit out of each other.

What was frantic at first becomes searching as we explore each other. His pecs have the slightest definition and just the right amount of fur that is sexy as hell. While his stomach's not hard ridges, there's a defined happy trail that has me salivating, just like the softness of his flesh and skin.

Light spills across him from the floor lamp. It highlights the contours of his body, catches the glint of a few silver hairs that intermingle with the chestnut brown.

Will's strong hand palms my ass, tearing a groan out of me and tugging me closer to him so we're side by side and grinding against each other. I've never been so grateful for the oversized couch. Desire floods through me, fogging my brain as I focus on nothing but the feel of him. The sensation of his touch.

And then we're unbuckling our belts, unzipping our pants, and I'm here for every whimper of anticipation.

A hand on my cock. A light squeeze. A tug. I groan into Will's mouth as he swipes a finger over the pearl of precum he's drawn from me. "Fuck." The word spills from me with a plunge of my hips. The grip he has on me tightens before he swipes his finger again, smoothing in the wetness providing the slightest bit of lube.

I part my mouth, drinking in his kisses as I angle away, parting us a little more so I can reach him fully. I need his weight in my hand. Am desperate to feel the vein I'm sure is pulsing under his velvety, smooth skin.

A stroke and touch and I find it, tracing the vein with the pads of my fingers.

Will gasps into my mouth, and I ease away and peer down at him.

Blown pupils stare up at me, and when shove his pants a little further down his hips, I wrap my fingers around his hard length. A shudder racks his body, and his lips part when I start moving.

He mimics the slide of my hand, having momentarily paused when I gripped him.

And it's on.

We're all tongue, teeth, rapidly moving palms. Groans, moans, grunts, and "Fuck yeses."

The tingle in my balls starts, drawing them up. On the cusp of exploding, I suck on the tender skin between Will's neck and shoulder before warning, "I'm going to fucking explode."

He nods rapidly, the movement unhinged, his hand on my cock unforgiving and so perfect. A garbled "Fuck" spills out of him right along with his load.

The wet heat on my skin has me bucking. Once, twice, and I'm there.

Blinding white spots dance in my vision as we shudder together, clinging to each other as I collapse. Our pants are loud in the quiet room. The sound caresses my skin, and I bottle up the moment, the sensation.

I can barely catch my breath.

"You doing okay there?"

I angle and lift up to see Will's face and the slow smile lifting his thoroughly kissed lips. But it's the teasing, the sated, doe-eyed look he's sending my way that has my heart tripping over itself.

It takes me a moment to get my brain working enough to answer him. "In my defense, cardio isn't part of my usual routine."

A laugh shakes his chest, and since I'm still half on top of him, nothing but cum and sweat between us—our pants and boxers around our ankles—I feel his amusement in every limb. It feels amazing, and I'm going to be honest, a relief.

This, the two of us sharing handjobs and the hottest of kisses, was nowhere in my plan of what we'd be doing later when I saw him in the coffee shop. Was that just this morning? It feels like a life-time ago. I suppose hours of conversation, laughter, shooting the shit—and the ball—and then shared orgasms can really make a man lose all sense of time.

But the relief is really focused on Will still being here, laughing and relaxed and not running. Not that he's given me any indication he'd do such a thing, but there've been a couple of moments today that his mind seemed elsewhere.

"Perhaps we just need more practice. We'll get both our fitness up in no time."

Surprise has me widening my eyes, ridiculously so, judging from the scrunching of Will's brow and the shine disappearing from his smile.

"But not if you don't want—"

"I want," I say quickly, perhaps a little too desperately. The orgasm was epic, for sure, but the time we spent together today was what made it the best day I've had in such a long time, and I'm eager to have more.

"You do?" Vulnerability trembles in his tone, and I hate that I put it there.

"Definitely do." I lean in close and press my mouth to his, teasing his lips and savoring his taste. It's so easy to get lost in his kisses. He uses just the right amount of tongue to get my dick twitching again—no small feat the older I'm getting.

When he smiles against my mouth, I angle away, drinking in the sight of him. "So we're both on board with building stamina on and off the court?"

I chuckle at the lightness in his tone and his bouncing brows. "Maybe on the sidelines of the court. Not sure I can handle playing so much these days."

"You're younger than me, right?" Humor laces his words.

"Maybe." I shrug, easing down to lean on my elbow and rest my cheek on my palm. "I turned thirty in March. You?"

"Thirty-nine last January."

"Ooh… the big four-oh next year. How are you feeling about that development? Any big plans?" What I don't do is gush over how fucking amazing he looks. Not that forty is old—not to me these days. But still, I legit thought he was in his early thirties when I first met him. Sure, Mav's ten, but that doesn't really give any true perspective on Will's age.

Something shifts in his expression, an emotion I can't quite name, but I wish it wasn't there. He purses his lips, and I feel like I should apologize even though I have no idea why. Instead, I change the subject, focusing on the mess we're covered in and how sticky I'm feeling.

"Perhaps the only plan we need right now is cleaning up. Shower?"

He bobs his head, and I exhale in relief. It seems to have been the perfect out for him, especially after that quiet moment.

"Come on, then. Let me see how clean I can get you before dirtying you right back up again."

Kicking my clothes free, I stand and reach out, a little giddy when he places his hand in mine with no hesitation and a light chuckle.

"Thirty-nine, remember."

Smirking when I realize the direction of his thoughts, I drop my gaze to his soft cock, my imagination already running wild at the thought of swallowing him down while he's soft and feeling him growing hard while in my mouth.

His dick twitches, and my attention snaps up. Eyes full of heat stare back at me. There's no holding back my satisfied smirk as I say, "Somehow I don't think that's going to be a problem."

It's not.

By the time we step out of the shower, my legs are like Jell-O and exhaustion rides me. It's the best kind of tired, though. A self-satisfied grin stretches across my lips as I reach my bed, only for my lip to curl at its stripped status.

I could kick myself for thinking it was a good idea to wash my sheets this morning.

"You okay there?"

I peer over at Will, catching the humor in his gaze as he stares at me. "I should have made my bed before showering." I'm totally being presumptuous here, but from the two orgasms, it seems natural to be heading to bed together.

His gaze drifts to the bed and rakes over the stripped mattress, but rather than a scrunched frown like I'm wearing, a smirk appears. "Totally worth bypassing making your bed to spend the time with you in the shower." He glances at my bedroom door. "We should probably take a look at your couch, though."

I huff out a laugh and shake my head. Will is refreshing as fuck. Not only is he funny when we're chatting and chilling, but there's no awkwardness, no shying away from what we just shared. "There's no arguing that."

"Come on. I'll help you clean up and make up the bed."

I'm not even surprised by his offer.

The couch just needs a wipe down—thank you, leather cushions.

Back in my bedroom, we soon make fast work of remaking the bed. By the time we're manhandling the last two pillowcases, we've talked about the ridiculous pleasure of having fresh sheets on the bed, especially after showering, and have moved on to the merits of a bath versus a shower.

"I can't even remember the last time I had a bath." I plump the pillow cover and try to straighten it out.

"It was the first thing I added to the house when I had it remodeled before moving in." Will throws the pillow to the top of the bed. "Mammoth thing with jets. It's ugly as sin, but hell if it isn't heaven." His grin is wide.

I chuckle. "So you got an ugly bath just because it makes bubbles?"

He snorts. "Yep. Also because Mav was only five at the time, and submerging him in water and distracting him with bath toys was the only way to get the grime off him." Loud laughter follows his words.

"Sounds like you had your hands full."

"Always, but it's the best kind of way to be busy. Even worth the countless number of hours I've had to spend mopping the bathroom floor." There's a touch of whimsy in his voice. Happy memories for me to read clear as day in his soft smile and faraway look.

"Well, with you now having a basketball pro on your hands, at least you won't need to worry about caked mud after games and practice like you would with football," I tease, positioning the pillow on my bed. "That's gotta help save the world or something, right? All that water not going down the drain?"

"You'd think that, huh? But I swear Mav just has to look at dirt and it magically latches onto him. Kel—" He clamps his jaw shut, his eyes widening a fraction as the color leeches from his face.

I have no idea what just happened, but gut deep I know asking him if he's okay or what's wrong isn't the right move. When I stand, his attention slams into me. "Food?" I ask. "You kind of distracted me when I was getting us fed."

Relief floods his features. "Yeah. Food sounds great."

Taking it as a win that he's not making a run for it, I tug on an old Minnesota Eagles tee, courtesy of Cassius, and a pair of shorts, offering sweatpants and a clean tee to Will. He grabs them gratefully, and I get a kick out of the sweatpants pooling around his feet. While I'm not a giant in basketball circles, compared to the average guy, I'm tall.

With twitching lips, I peer at Will. "They fit well."

A sardonic eyebrow lift and stare is sent my way. "That right?"

"Well, they're not quite as tight around your junk as the gray sweats you were weari—"

"Fuck off." He huffs out the words with a laugh. "They were the only pair I had."

"And I'm very grateful for the fact," I tease as he rolls his eyes and follows me to the kitchen. "I'm serious."

"Uh-huh."

"Yup. I think there needs to be a uniform regulation for hot dads."

A snort and a slight elbow check from Will and I grin. "You're incorrigible." He shakes his head and stops before the abandoned food.

"I am that." I take a slow, deliberate perusal of his broad chest, all the way down to my gray pants that frame a sizable bulge. He's not quite hard, but even when soft, his size is impressive.

The clearing of his throat jerks my attention up. "So I just destroy my ten-year-old sweats, then?" His eyes are alight with mischief, and considering fifteen minutes ago, I swallowed his cum in the shower, I like how at ease we are together. There's no painful awkwardness. No desperate need to get him out of my space.

"Fuck no. That would be a tragedy. In fact, I think gray sweatpants should be the only item of clothing you wear when we're together." Before we showered, the discussion had teased at us seeing each other again, but I want to put it out there front and center.

Does it make me come across as desperate?

Fuck if I know or care.

I'm going off gut instinct here. Okay, and maybe a bit of post-coital bliss. Regardless, I like the guy, and from the memory of his cum face and the way he's nibbling on the olive while his gaze sets me on fire, I'm fairly certain he's enjoying spending time with me too.

"I expect there'll be a formal complaint or two if I wear those sweatpants again at practice. Once I got away with. Twice—"

"And the practice will start to be inundated by parents panting over the hot coach dad."

A blush blooms at my words, and he can barely meet my eyes. Jesus H. Christ, this man is sweet hotness in the flesh.

"Maybe you should stick with wearing sweatpants while you're here." I wink. "Wouldn't want you to be distracted by having to fend off all those admirers. Not that I don't like a little healthy competition every now and then."

He huffs out an amused breath and rolls his eyes. "Now I know you're just talking shit. I've been back in town for five years, and I'm pretty damn sure I'm not at risk of needing a bodyguard to defend my virtue."

And isn't that an interesting nugget of information. Bubbles pop in my gut at the implication of him choosing me. Because despite what he's said, I doubt very much that countless men and women in town, and most likely from neighboring communities who visit the coffeeshop, don't want to take a bite.

We focus on piling our plates with the meats, cheeses, and olives I left out. Thankfully, with fall edging closer, it brings with it chilly evenings and mornings, so us abandoning the food hasn't resulted in anything being spoiled.

"Okay to eat on our laps and watch something on TV?" It's only just after eight, but I'm aware I've stolen Will away practically all day. Since we weren't originally getting together until six, I'm hopeful it means he doesn't need or want to duck out any time soon.

It would be tragic not to mess up my clean sheets.

"Sounds good. There's a couple of new Prime movies I've yet had the chance to watch."

Smiling, knowing he's happy to hang out for at least another couple of hours, we head to my living room and sit side by side on the couch. There're still empty beer bottles on the coffee table and empty snack bowls from the potato chips we demolished earlier. It reminds me we haven't got fresh drinks.

"Another beer or something else?"

"Maybe water." He glances at me. "I'm pretty much sobered up, so it makes sense to stay that way."

"Water it is." After collecting the water jug from the fridge, I swipe two glasses and head back to Will.

Sobering up is a good thing. The reality is, Collier's Creek is a fairly small town. While we have neighboring feeder towns that make up a decent proportion of our kids at the high school, and it's one of those places that now I know Will, I expect I'll be seeing him at every turn.

There's also Maverick to consider. I'm the kid's coach. I'll be with his dad while spending time with the team. All that means is, making sober decisions and already not having a single ounce of regret for the day we've shared together is a good thing.

As for Maverick…. Well, Will is a grown-ass man. I trust that he knows what he's doing. From the sounds of it, he doesn't make rash decisions, and hopefully ones that he does make, he doesn't live to regret. It means I'll follow his lead. That doesn't mean I won't eagerly hope and make clear that I want to see where this spark between us goes.

CHAPTER SIX

WILL

IF I DIDN'T KNOW ANY BETTER, I'D THINK I'D BEEN blessed—or cursed. I suppose it all depends on the perspective.

Not only have I met someone who I enjoy spending adult time with, a man who I can laugh and joke and be myself with who's also an honest-to-god decent human being. But he's also incredible with Mav and the whole team. He's firm but fair, and he genuinely wants the kids to have a good time.

He's also super understanding of our limited time together.

Who am I kidding?

It's more like the nonexistent time we have. The last three times we've attempted to make something happen and meet up, I've had to cancel twice, then

Colton canceled our plan for a catch-up two nights ago.

Hence me wondering if I'm actually cursed.

How am I meant to really get to know a guy and see if there's the possibility of more if we never get a break? It's not even as if I can blame my career.

It's been over five years since I had a late night at work. Over five years since I felt the stress and pressure of meeting a deadline. It was a lifetime ago, another world even, when I ran my firm side by side with my business partner, Tony.

Now I work incredible hours of just nine to three during the weekdays in a job I don't technically need. I'm blessed. I get it. I also worked my ass off since college with my startup cybersecurity company, which led me to the point of being able to walk away as a silent business partner while still picking up healthy dividends that most hardworking people could only dream about.

But still, all of that doesn't stop me from having a pity party. Which then makes me feel like an ungrateful dick.

There's one easy way out of the predicament of finding time for Colton, but "easy" is bullshit. Telling Mav I want to spend time with the coach he adores so I can get to know him better and possibly date him is not going to happen.

Not yet.

Hell, maybe not ever.

How can I bring someone into my boy's life if I'm not sure there's a real future?

The answer is I simply can't.

But I really want this connection I feel with Colton to pan out. The fact that he's the first person I've spent time with—let alone kissed and shared orgasms with—since Kelly means something. Of that I am certain.

"Are you even listening to me?"

Mom sounds concerned more than annoyed, so I quickly plaster on a smile that isn't too difficult to fix in place and nod. "Dad's determined to convince Elle that something extra special is needed for this year's annual Jake Day." I can't help the lip twitch. For years I escaped the festivities of the fall Jake Day celebrations, but since being back, it's clear that they have grown in my absence.

Not only is it a big day for the locals as we celebrate Jake Collier, the town's founder, but it's one of the last days of the season to bring tourists—and therefore money—into the town before the crazy blizzards we experience over winter.

Mom narrows her gaze, not sure how much I was really paying attention. Obviously she's right, since mooning over Colton means I haven't been fully focused.

"Doesn't Elle love helping out, though, when folks around here let him?" While I'm wealthy, Elle is old-money wealthy. And despite his reputation of being a busybody and frustrating some folks in town, his heart's in a good place.

"Yes, but it's what your father wants to do that's the problem."

"Which is?"

Mom tuts. "I knew you weren't listening."

I press my lips together, marveling at how Mom can still scold me despite me being almost forty. Instead of defending myself, I shrug, much like I did as a kid.

"He wants to dress up as Jake in his ridiculous getup and jump out of a plane after it's done that skywriting thing."

"He what?" I puff out my lips, catching my laughter. Mom is deadly serious, and my laughing at Dad's antics is likely to push her over the edge. Or more likely have her asking questions about why I think it's an awesome idea if Mav stays over tonight for another sleepover. Given that it's only been two weeks since the last time, she'll already be suspicious.

"You need to talk to him. I swear that man gets more stubborn the grayer he gets."

I bob my head, agreeing with her. He's always been a stubborn goat, but since he retired a few years back, he digs in his heels even more. Though, in his defense, it tends to be when Mom's trying to get him to join her for ballroom lessons or Swedish lessons or whatever else they have going on at the town hall.

"I'm pretty sure they have policies in place for people with medical conditions. I can't imagine anyone letting Dad jump out of an airplane." At least I hope not. Between his high blood pressure and the heart attack he had seven years back, he's not quite fighting fit. Knowing Dad, I imagine he's simply trying to get a rise out of Mom.

When I realize Mom's staring at me, I bob my head, saying, "But yes, I'll talk to him if it'll make you feel better."

"Thank you." Apparently, that's all she needed to hear, as she gets back to rolling out the cookie dough.

"Anytime."

She flicks her gaze at me, a soft smile forming on

her lips. "Are you leaving that grandson of mine with us tonight?"

I wait a beat, not wanting to sound too eager that she brought it up. "I suppose. If Mav wants to." I'm already wondering how quickly I can text Colton to see if he's available. Mom and Dad were due to head out of town this weekend for a fiftieth-anniversary party, but it was canceled last minute due to an unfortunate injury involving enthusiastic sex and chocolate paste. As soon as Dad had chuckled through the story, I'd tried to shut it down, equally horrified and fascinated by what their friends had been getting up to.

"He's already asked."

"He has?" News to me, but I love that my boy has such a great relationship with my parents. And that he wants to spend time with them is wonderful. I know Mom and Dad are eager to get as much time with him as possible before he's too busy hanging out with his friends or interested in dating.

"Your dad's out there setting up the tent."

Courtesy of their manipulative grandson they dote on, I suspect. I love that for him, and for Mom and Dad as well.

"What will you get into tonight? Another boys'

night with Coach Green who I keep hearing so much about?"

I will not blush. I will not—

"Why've you gone all red?" Pausing her cookie cutting, Mom stares at me hard. A couple of beats later, her eyebrows shoot high. "Oh…."

"It's not—"

"William Wyatt Evans." When Mom full names me, I always listen. I also quickly shut my mouth and wait patiently while trying not to melt into an embarrassed puddle. "Whether you believe it or not, I know you inside and out."

It's true that even though I spent years away at college and then running my company and starting a family thousands of miles from home, we've remained close. I'm pretty sure she still knows all my tells.

"There's never a need to lie to me or play anything down. You know your heart and mind better than any other person I know." Her unwavering gaze dares me to attempt to challenge her. Unsurprisingly I don't, nor do I need to. "You give every single piece of yourself to make sure my grandson is happy."

Warmth swells in my chest, emotion following swiftly behind.

"That you're still working when you've no need to is admirable."

I swallow hard as she speaks, struggling to hear her words of praise without breaking down. I don't want to get caught up in high emotion.

Life's been better in recent years. The days are filled with my son's laughter, sunshine, a few blizzards, and growing acceptance. Sure, the nights in a quiet house have always been more difficult, but they're getting easier.

"That you're still working in order to show Maverick what a work ethic looks like—" She shakes her head. "You make me proud every single day."

"Mom—" My attempt at shutting her love fest down is a fail.

"Every. Single. Day."

"I know. Thank you," I whisper.

"So give yourself grace to be happy again. For more than Maverick," she adds before I get the chance to argue with her about how much happiness my son brings into my world. "Find someone to spend your time with if you're ready to put yourself out there. Open yourself to finding a happiness that's just for you. It's okay to fall in love again. Kelly wanted that for you."

I hold my breath and count to ten. Tears have

kept me company so often since losing Kelly to breast cancer, but being wrung out isn't how I want to start my evening. It's also not something I want Mav seeing, not when everything is going so great.

"I know." There's a catch in my voice despite my determination to keep my emotions at bay. The cancer spread so quickly that one moment Kelly was being diagnosed, and six weeks later, I was planning her funeral. The shock and devastation had reverberated in my soul, Mav the only reason I kept standing.

Six weeks had at least been enough time for Kelly to settle her affairs and to tell me in that sharp, determined, take-no-shit way of hers that she wanted me to find love, fall hard, and become a family with whoever was lucky enough to steal my heart and our son's.

In one of the numerous letters she'd left behind, she'd reiterated the same thing.

Kelly had been nothing if not doggedly stubborn and had the determination of a relentless river, one carving its way through the Wyoming mountains surrounding my small town.

And fuck if I didn't still love her for it. I always would.

"Good." Mom wipes her hands on a towel and

steps toward me. "Whatever you need, we're here—me and your parachute-jumping father."

I snort, grateful for her breaking the tension. "Thanks, Mom."

"And if things with this Coach Green or whomever else you find yourself drawn to pans out, we'll be eager to meet them."

I let slip, "Only time will tell," happy to give her at least something. How can I not when she gives me and Mav so much love and support?

"Glad to hear it." She presses a kiss on my cheek and squeezes my forearm before retreating. "Right, be sure to have a quick word with your dad before you make your escape."

"Will do." I pocket my keys and head to the back door, stopping when Mom calls my name. "Yeah?" I ask, turning to look at her.

"It's Friday night, so if tonight happens to turn into a weekend, just shoot me a message. Mav will be more than happy to spend two nights with his mamaw and pops."

Once again, heat floods me, and I haul ass to escape my mom's not-so-quiet chuckling.

Shaking off disappointment sucks, but I've totally got this. That Colton didn't pick up my call or respond to my message about meeting tonight shouldn't make me feel so lousy, but after Mom's talk and building up in my head how great it will be to finally get together with Colton again, I kind of set myself up.

But I'm determined to suck it up and at least try to have a decent night.

I tug open the door to Jake's Tap. Loud conversation, laughter, and the clink of glasses greet me. My shoulders relax. At least here there'll be people I know. While I've rarely been out since returning to Collier's Creek, the locals in this bar tend to be multiple generations of Collier residents. It means I'll know most of the patrons here, so even if I wanted to be alone while I knocked back a beer, it's highly unlikely I will be.

There's a band setting up in the corner of the room. Four guys stand around, one with a guitar in hand, another seems to be tuning a bass, another twirling drumsticks. But it's the fourth man who has my eyes widening in surprise.

I veer away from the bar counter, my gaze glued to the side profile of Jason. A grin splits my mouth just before I call out, "They'll let any punk in this joint."

The bearded guy to Jason's right snaps his attention to me, his eyes hard. A split second later, Jason angles my way, his lips quirking. "Only punks who know how to save skinny runts from being pummeled in the field." He shakes his head and drags me into a hug. "Fuck, man."

I grunt as he squeezes me hard.

"The hell you doing here?" Jason grabs hold of my shoulders and pulls back to look at me.

"Been back a few years now. More to the point, what the hell are you doing here?" Jason looks every bit the rock star he always promised he'd be. With a shaggy haircut that should look ridiculous on him, since he's thirty-eight years old, he's rocking the style. The torn jeans and the black fitted tee suit him, but fuck, how is it that he looks so much more than a year younger than me?

"I'm not sure a single beer, hell, one conversation, will be enough for that story, but if you're hanging around, we can definitely catch up."

"Definitely."

The guy who gave me a death stare a moment ago doesn't appear like he wants to stab me, but he still looks wary as he eyes me up and down.

I get it.

Since being back in Collier's Creek, I've embraced my inner small-town Wyoming. I'm dressed in Wrangler's, a button-down shirt, and while I'm not wearing cowboy boots, battered Timberlands finish the outfit. It's a long way from the pressed suits of my CEO days and a far cry from the rock-god look Jason's owning.

"I've got thirty minutes before we're due to play. Why not hook a guy up with a draft of the local stuff first, then we catch up properly later?" Jason passes the death-glare guy a mic, a silent exchange and a quirked eyebrow passing between them.

"Yeah, sure," I say, already taking a couple of steps back. The man at his side shoots me a pissed-off glare, which is my cue to back on out of there and not get between whatever that is.

I order us a couple of local draft beers and manage to snag the last two seats at the end of the wooden bar. It's crowded tonight. With Jason playing, I understand why. The last I'd heard was, he'd made it big and was playing festivals, then sold-out concerts. His band's music still played regularly on the radio. But at least ten years have passed by since I'd heard any new music from him. Not that I'm a music buff, nor have I searched or wondered where he'd got to.

Life while being a new dad and running a company had been too busy to keep up with any of my school friends. We'd all moved on. But here Jason is, playing music with a band, and in Jake's Tap of all places.

It isn't exactly Red Rocks Amphitheater.

"Thank fuck." Jason slams onto the barstool next to me, his shoulder brushing mine because of how close we're having to sit. I should probably order a couple more drinks now before it gets even busier. He swipes his beer and gulps down several mouthfuls, only stopping when there's less than half left and he has a lip of foam.

"Better?" I chuckle and indicate toward his lip.

His grin is wide and makes him look even more like the young guy who really did save my ass on the field more times than I can count. Swiping his mouth, he puts down his glass and clasps me on the shoulder. "Man, it's good to see you. Seriously. I can't believe you moved back to town."

My shrug is light, trying for carefree as I take a gulp of my beer. A burst of bubbles hits my tongue before I can appreciate the malty freshness. I focus on the taste, not wanting to get into my story. It's already been a day of reminiscing.

I settle on: "A few years now. Came back with my boy, Mav. He's ten now."

"Shit, a kid." He shakes his head in wonder, and I can assume from that reaction, he doesn't have any of his own. "Congrats, man."

I laugh. It's been a while since I've been congratulated on having a child. "Thanks. He's the best. Just started playing basketball, though." My wince is fake and earns me the snicker I was hoping for.

"Well, you can't win 'em all," he jests, his voice loud as the volume spikes.

I glance around at the bodies. The place is crammed. "How about you?" I all but yell despite Jason's nearness. "When was the last time you came back to Collier's? It must have been a while."

A few twangs of a guitar pierce the air and grab our attention. The scowling guitar player's eyes are on us.

Jason sighs. "I'm being summoned." He adds an eye-roll for good measure. He leans in closer, the noise of the bar forcing him to do so. "Definitely don't leave after the set. We've g—"

"Hey, I'm not interrupting, am I?"

I jerk my head at the question, my smile immediate. Colton. He's within touching distance. Not a surprise with how maxed out the bar is.

"You're here. You came." I reach out instinctively, take his hand, and pull him the extra inches closer. On contact, a smile splits his cheeks, and he comes willingly.

He leans in. "And you're here?" Questions fill his gaze.

Before I can respond, a loud rap of knuckles appears on the bar next to me. It's Jason. "If you're busy later—"

"No, I'll still be around," I say immediately. There's something in his tone that has me offering. With Colton here, we won't have the chance for a proper catch-up, but we can at least exchange numbers and can arrange another time to meet if he wants.

Jason's gaze flicks to Colton, his gaze assessing. He dips his attention to my hand on Colton's waist, which I don't even remember putting there. But I have no desire to pull away. "Good." He smiles at Colton, all wide-mouthed and bad-boy charming, before he throws him a ridiculously flirtatious wink. "You two enjoy the set."

With a chin up-nod, he walks away, pushing through the crowd, saying high to familiar faces along the way. Colton pulling away snags my full focus. I frown before I realize he's claiming the stool beside me.

I move in close so he can hear and ask, "How'd you know I'd be here?"

He shakes his head. "I didn't. Didn't even know you'd be out."

The disappoint that had sat heavily on my chest earlier fizzles away. "I called and texted, wanting to let you know Mav's with my parents tonight."

All weekend if we want.

I keep that to myself, not wanting to be too pushy and also not wanting to say it aloud. The words sound a little shitty—the idea of me celebrating being without my son. But that's so not it.

Okay, maybe it's a little bit that too. But only because the chance to be the Will who's not just a dad doesn't happen very often, and it's taken me a long time to convince myself it's okay to have moments of separation while enjoying the time out.

"That'll explain it. I spent the afternoon at work, catching up with some planning and making sure I had what I need for some lessons next week. I ended up leaving my phone in my lab. Couldn't be bothered to head back in to grab it." He shrugs. "If I'd have known, I would have made the effort."

Warmth settles in my chest. Sure, he could be bullshitting and simply be an outrageous flirt, but that doesn't quite gel with the man I've got to know over the past month. "So what brought you out?" Shit. The question freezes my breath. Is he here with someo— I cut the thought off immediately, internally rolling my eyes at myself.

He's sitting right next to you, asshole.

"Heard there was a band playing. Didn't think you were available, and I really needed to escape from the pile of grading sitting on my dining room table."

"Well, I'm glad you found me." I ease away so I can look him in the eyes, wanting him to see how genuine my words are.

"Me too."

CHAPTER SEVEN

COLTON

The band's good. Different from what I expected when first seeing Jason, the guy who I've learned is an old high school teammate of Will's. He screams rock. Not with his vocals, which I'd expected, just his dark, broody sex-god looks.

There's no denying he's hot as fuck.

There's also no denying that when I saw him with his tongue almost in Will's ear, it had hurt. I'd been temporarily frozen when I first spotted Will. Jake's Tap was the last place I'd expected to see him tonight. Add in the gorgeous black-haired guy, and I'd wondered what the hell I'd walked into.

For a split second, I'd contemplated fleeing. I had no rights to Will's attention. Sure, we'd had one incredible day and night together. The sex had been phenomenal. And while we'd tried to spend time together off the court, since we'd never managed to get our schedules aligned, we weren't officially anything to each other.

Thank fuck I thought better of it, reminded myself I wasn't a jealous schmuck, and went to say hello.

The way his smile had lit his face, the speed with which he'd greeted me and tugged me close, was totally worth it. I figure it was my reward for not backing away and reading into something without knowing the facts.

Jason and his band are playing their last song. Well, it's a slow number that's at odds with the whole band's look, but Jason's gruff voice sings the shit out of it. I haven't heard the song before, so maybe it's an original.

"They're good," I say.

Will nods. "He always has been. Was the lead singer of Crimson Fury for about a decade or so."

Surprise has me jerking my head back to Jason. The mic's close to his mouth and his eyes are closed as he belts out lyrics about heartache and cruel twists of fate. Crimson Fury were huge when I was in high school and college. I haven't really considered there's not been any new music from them that

I'm aware of. I assume it's just the nature of the game. Bands and artists are hot until, for whatever reason, they're not.

"What's he doing playing here?"

Will shrugs. "No idea. We said we'd catch up after the set."

I don't want to offer, but it feels shitty not to. Reluctantly, and desperately hoping he shuts me down, I ask, "Do you need me to head out and leave you to it so you can catch up?"

God, I love his smile. It's soft and sweet, and even in the dim lighting of the bar, I can tell he likes that I offered.

"No, definitely not. I'll make sure I grab his number. And if he's in town for a while, we can meet up another time. Thank you, though." He brushes his thumb on my back, something he's been doing off and on over the last couple of hours. That we're forced to sit so close is a blessing. I can happily handle all the loudness and volume of bodies if it makes it easier for us to touch.

"Okay, good." I flick my focus back to the band as Jason's voice lifts. There's a punch to the pitch, the song building. "And after," I say, angling back to Will, "you want to come over and stay the night?"

I wait for embarrassment to set in, not used to

being quite so bold these days. But with our failed attempts at spending alone time together, I don't want to miss this opportunity.

Do I want to hook up? Fuck yes. My dick is absolutely on board. But if all he wants to do is talk and sleep, maybe even cuddle, I'm not adverse to that either. Hell, if any of my old friends heard me even admitting that, they'd wonder what had happened to the ballsy small forward who had a mighty fine time playing the proverbial field in college.

"I'd love to." His hand moves to my neck, and he squeezes lightly. The touch sends ripples of awareness down my spine, and I desperately hope my assumption that this is the last song being played is right.

The final few chords fill the bar, and loud applause breaks out. Whistles and cheers are close to blowing the roof off. We join in, but I kind of wish Will would return to touching my neck or back. Hell, any part of me he wishes that we can get away with in public.

He does make it difficult to remember to behave like the professional I am when he's close by and his hands are on me. Tricky when I've already spotted at least a couple of parents of kids I teach.

The joy of teaching and living in a small town.

By the time Jason and his bandmates have wrapped up and Jason seems to have spoken to at least half of the locals who'd come out to watch him play, we've had another beer, and I'm well on my way to being buzzed.

Fortunately, at the end of the set, most of the crowd cleared out, and since it's close to last call, it seems like only a few of the regulars remain. Being able to hear myself speak is a shock to the system, and my ears are ringing.

Will stands when his friend approaches. They hug and pat each other's backs. "You guys were incredible." He reaches over and shakes the hands of the other guys. "Seriously, I can't remember the last time I heard live music, and you all were phenomenal."

Sweat trickles down Jason's temple. How does he make sweating look sexy? Though, I think Will could pull it off. A flash of a similar drip of sweat when we jacked each other off slams into me, and I smirk to myself.

Yeah, he can definitely pull it off.

"Thanks, man. Let me introduce you to the guys." Before he does, he says a quick thanks to Jodi who's appeared with fresh drinks. "This here is Tommy, Noel, and Xavier." The three other members of the band bob their heads in greeting as they eagerly accept the beers Will passes over.

"Impressive set tonight," Will says, and I bob my head in agreement.

"Have you played together long?" While I don't know much about Crimson Fury, from the looks of the young drummer who can't be older than twenty-five, I figure this isn't the original band.

Actually, I don't think I heard what their band name is. Maybe Jason isn't the lead singer or guitarist of Crimson Fury anymore, and if he isn't, does that mean the band packed up shop?

It's Noel, the guitarist, who says, "About three years now, just honing our sound. I played with Jase years back with Crimson when Carlisle was MIA."

"I didn't catch your band name," I admit.

"Echoes of Granite," Jason answers, and he throws a wink at the young drummer. "Courtesy of the kid over here."

Tommy flips him off. "What can I say, I've got brains as well as skills."

The guys laugh, all except Xavier, the bass player. He rolls his eyes and looks completely disinterested.

"Jase said the two of you played football together," Tommy asks after taking a huge gulp of beer.

"A million years ago, yeah."

"Fuck, Will," Jason all but splutters, "don't give the kid any more fuel by saying shit like that. You're making us sound like fossils."

Will snorts out a laugh, and I smile at the sound, loving that he's so relaxed and amused. What I'd prefer, though, is to hurry this catch-up session along so I can take him home and peel his clothes off.

The last two weeks have been torture. Standing beside the man while he patiently helps our ragtag team of players, I have to actively focus on anything but him. If not, it's all too easy to lean in a little too close, for my voice to turn to gravel when a smile makes his eyes sparkle or he bends, revealing glutes I want to bite into.

The conversation has moved on to Will regaling Jason's bandmates with stories of their lead singer when he was in high school. I chuckle along, my fingers having a mind of their own as I play with the hair at the nape of Will's neck.

It's only as I glance at the group and notice Xavier's hard, curious stare on my hand that I realize what I'm doing and pause.

Sure, Will's been touchy-feely tonight. It doesn't mean I'm not super aware of the possibility of the gossip mill already picking up on that with rumors spreading far and wide by tomorrow. Not that I'm concerned about me, but my concern about Will, and more specifically Mav, hasn't changed.

Will turning to look at me gets my attention. His brow's dipped low, and it's obvious he's wondering why I stopped pawing at him. "You okay?"

I bob my head and flick my attention to Xavier. His eyes are on me, and while I intended a quick glance, I can't look away and leave this alone. "Something wrong, Xavier?" I keep the bite out of my question. I've spent over ten years wrangling surly teenagers. I know how to handle a moody bass player.

If he's surprised I've called him out, he doesn't show it. He pulls a face that says, "No, not really." Do I buy it? Hell no. But I'm not fazed either.

"For fuck's sake, Xavier." Rather than pissed, Jason sounds resigned. "They're together, obviously. Now stop being a prick." The shake of his head seems like something he's done a million times before. "Ignore him," Jason says to me and Will. "The only thing he knows how to interact with is his bass."

Tommy cackles and bobs his head. "It's true. He's also gay as fuck and was just making sure no one was hitting on Jason."

"The fuck?" Jason shouts while Xavier grunts, "Was not, you fuckhead."

Delight fills Tommy's expression as he's no doubt loving getting a rise out of his two bandmates. A quick glance at Noel, who appears half asleep as he lazily looks through his phone, and it's clear he's not paying a lick of attention to Tommy's words or Jason and Xavier's impassioned denial.

What do I think? Tommy may be onto something, sure, but also, if he is and Xavier is gay and isn't out… like, what the fuck? Once again, I can't keep my mouth shut. In my defense, Tommy is young enough that I could have been his teacher. "Outing someone is never okay." I'm in total teacher mode, keeping my voice steady, the underlying quiet disapproval clear in my tone.

Tommy lifts his palms in the air in a placating gesture. The smug smile he's sporting doesn't look like he's feeling the least bit guilty, though.

Not sure how to respond or deal with the weird tension in the air, I keep quiet and practically sag when Will jumps in, saying, "Colton and I are about to head out. You in town for a couple of days?"

Jason bobs his head and tugs out his phone. "Give me your digits, and we'll meet up."

They exchange details while I stand, knock back

my beer, and am practically dancing from foot to foot while waiting for them to say goodbye. Tonight's been unexpectedly great. With the exception of the weird last few minutes, I'm eager to finish off this night with alone time with Will.

"Sorry if I put you on edge before."

I jolt at the closeness of the voice, not expecting it or realizing Xavier was so close. His dark eyes are impenetrable midnight ink, and while he still looks murderous, I think I'm safe, since I'm receiving an unexpected apology. "All good."

He bobs his head. "Tommy's young and hyper, but he usually means well. He also has a big mouth."

I chuckle. "I've taught lots of kids like him over the years."

"You're a braver man than me."

"That's one way of putting it. Foolish is another acceptable word," I say lightly.

"And Tommy, what he said, well, thanks for saying what you did. He doesn't think sometimes. I'm also out, so it's no big deal."

I clamp my mouth shut, not exactly agreeing with his "no big deal" comment, but if he feels that way, it's completely his prerogative. It's tempting to ask about the other tidbit Tommy said, but Will's "You ready?" stops me.

Probably just as well.

"Yeah, sure," I say with a smile before turning back to the band. "It was good meeting you all."

We say our goodbyes, and Will and I head out, waving goodbye to Jodi. Her eyes are on our joined hands, her brows bouncing when she makes eye contact.

Yeah, news of Coach Green holding hands with the hot barista could possibly be all around town and school by Monday.

The cooling breeze touches my skin as soon as we step outside. Town is deserted, not surprising considering the time. It makes cuddling up to Will easier, since I'm super aware we need to have a more serious conversation at some point.

It sucks, really, the need to have grown-up discussions when you're in the early stages of getting to know someone. But it is what it is.

"Did you have a good time tonight?" Will tucks his palm into one of my back pockets, the move sweetly smooth and feeling all too natural.

"Yeah, the band was great. Company even better." I smirk down at him, catching his gaze. Sure, it's cheesy, but it's also true. I wrap my arm over his shoulder, drinking in his closeness. It's been a long time since I've felt this way—the excitement of starting something new.

Beyond one serious relationship that blew up about six years ago, it's been a series of dry spells, failed first dates, and casual hookups. A tingle of anticipation thrums through me. I want to grab onto the feeling and bottle it up.

But first.

I maneuver Will into the narrow alleyway between the library and the clinic.

"What the—"

I cut his question off with a kiss, eager to finally get my mouth on his after two weeks of not having a taste. I groan into his mouth, feeling his small smirk. Clearly I'm not doing this right if he has the ability to smile.

Stepping up my game, I hold him close, one palm on his cheek, the other on the small of his back. Warm and soft, his tongue strokes mine. When Will's breath hitches, I deepen the kiss, our mouths melding, all heat and passion and so much need, my gut tenses, my cock rising to the occasion.

The intensity increases as I grip him closer, our bodies pressing even tighter together. When his fingers glide against my back, lifting my shirt, stroking my skin, a wave of pleasure barrels through me.

It's time to move. To take this away from any possibility of getting caught. But fuck if stepping away isn't proving difficult. The friction is too good, so damn perfect.

"Fuck," I gasp, tearing my mouth from his. "We need to get rid of these clothes."

Will nods rapidly and fumbles for my hand in the near pitch-black. "Let's go."

I grin the whole way home despite the difficulty walking with tight jeans. Uncomfortable pants and a twenty-minute walk I plan to shorten to fifteen is going to be totally worth it.

CHAPTER EIGHT

WILL

Blessed quiet. The stillness is a little disconcerting for all of five seconds before I exhale in relief.

Colton's low chuckle reaches my ears. "You doing okay over there?"

I pick up the bulging bag of basketballs and face him with a smile. "I am now. Credit to you, doing this day in, day out."

A snort escapes as he shakes his head. "Well, not quite this. Sure, some of my senior classes act like some of these kids at times, but my days are usually less chaotic and not filled with balls flying in all directions." His mouth twitches when my eyebrow lifts. "And head out of the gutter," he whispers. The heat is there in his gaze, though, and fully directed at me.

"Completely your fault, that one," I challenge, already looking forward to the time I can kiss him senseless.

Last Friday's impromptu get-together turned into a weekend of slow and hot moments, complete with aching wrists and jaws. But more than that, we talked and laughed, discussed places we'd been, people we'd seen. While I still hadn't shared anything with him about Kelly, not quite ready for the look of sympathy I expected to be sent my way, we did talk about Mav.

We were definitely taking it fast behind closed doors, and Friday night I wasn't exactly shy at Jake's Tap, but we agreed to go a little slower with Mav. I also knew that before we dove even deeper, and definitely before we reached the point of sharing with Mav, Colton needed to know about Kelly.

Kelly isn't a dirty secret. Determined that Mav doesn't forget his mom, I talk about her with him all the time. I never want him to hold back or not feel comfortable. Bringing someone I'm seeing, maybe at some point dating, into the fold has to be timed right.

Or hell, I think that's the way it has to be.

Honestly, I'm making this shit up as I go. But beneath my second-guessing is a ten-year-old boy who's the center of my world. I know I have needs, deserve happiness, and everything else the internet tells a widower they are "allowed," but Mav is my priority.

That Colton understands and respects the need for baby steps is a hell of a thing. Reassuring, too, confirming he is so much more than a kick-ass basketball coach, a science nerd, and delectable kisser. He's caring and compassionate.

I'm starting to think he's the whole package. The combination makes me jittery.

"All done, Coach." Right on cue, as my kid has a special talent for cutting me off from sexy and serious thoughts, Mav bounds out of the storage room. His cheeks are no longer fire red from the shuttle runs—or at least a mini version of them. Instead, he looks to be buzzing with renewed energy.

Maybe he snuck in a candy bar or something. It's not normal, right, for anyone to bounce back so quickly?

"Great job, Mav. Thank you. I'm just about done here with your dad, too, so you can both escape and get out of here. Get a good meal in you."

"Dad said we can head to Fox's Restaurant tonight for burgers."

It didn't take too much convincing when Mav asked to go, especially knowing how a ninety-minute practice kicks my butt. Give me fourteen hours navigating through coding and a potload of coffee to fuel me, and I could keep going. Ninety minutes with a bunch of ten- and eleven-year-olds, and I felt every one of my thirty-nine years and then some.

"That sounds great. I've heard the burgers are the best in town." Colton's attention is fully on Mav. Admittedly, I love that. Interrupted in the middle of innuendo and flirting, but he doesn't miss a beat.

Mav's brow dips low, and I press my lips together at the look of horror morphing his features. "You haven't been to Fox's? But they're the best. You should totally come with us. Isn't that right, Dad? Coach has to try one of the burgers." He directs an adorable if not completely overexaggerated look of pleading my way.

I have no desire to argue with him or even give Colton an out if I can get away with it. More time with Colton? Sign me up.

I direct my gaze at Colton and am greeted with a small smirk. When he doesn't speak, his eyes on me,

I bob my head quickly. A little too enthusiastically. "You should definitely come if you don't have plans." Call me overeager and stick a bow on me, but these are the moments I crave. Mav and Colton getting to know each other off the court.

Not that I'm completely selfless. Snatched conversations when Mav's fast asleep are what I've been hanging on for every night since last weekend. It may have only been a few nights ago, but I want more time to get to know him. More opportunities for Mav to see he's a great man and so much more than the coach he thinks is the best.

I am super aware I'm the person standing in the way of making all of that happen faster. I'm nothing if not a walking contradiction.

"No plans." A crooked smile forms, but his unspoken questions are clear in his eyes. *Is this okay? Do you want this?*

"Perfect. We'd love for you to join us."

"Well, all right, then. Let's get this place locked up, and you guys can introduce me to Collier's finest burgers."

Mav's fist pump and "Yes" make my heart thunder. I seriously don't want to fuck this up for any of us, especially not him.

We leave in a convoy to the restaurant. Once

inside, Fiona leads us to a table. "You want to start off with drinks?" She smiles down at us, pad and pen in her hand.

"Mav?" I ask.

"Coke, please."

"Make that a Zero," I quickly add. I focus on Colton and tilt my head. Fuck, he's handsome. His eyes are just for me, and from the expression on his face, I can only imagine what he's thinking. The hint of a blush is sweet, though. "Colton, what about you?" I manage to ask, impressed with my steady voice.

"I'll have what Mav's having," he says, peering over at Fiona.

"Make that three, please, Fiona."

"Sure thing. I'll be right back with those. The specials are on the board. Let me know if you have any questions." Her grin is wide as she sweeps her gaze over us before she leaves us to it.

"So, the burger, Mav? Any particular one?" Colton peers over the menu at Mav.

My boy's eyes are wide and bright. He's always been a kid to help out and doesn't hold back on sharing his thoughts. And given that it's his coach asking, I expect he's buzzing and close to exploding with wanting to give Colton the best advice ever. "The works, Coach." His nod is so fast, I'm a little concerned for his brain rattling around. "Dad says it's the only way he can get me to eat some greens, and he's not wrong."

I snort out a laugh, and Colton's lips twitch.

"Hmm… what sort of greens? Now, if it was veggies, I'd be all over that."

On cue, Mav turns up his nose. He's nothing if not predictable, my boy. "Why would you want veggies anywhere near a burger?"

"Well…" Another lip twitch follows, but his eyes are full of intensity and fully focused on Mav. "When I was at college, I was this close"—he holds his thumb and pointer finger a couple of inches apart—"to going pro."

How did I not know that? I study Colton, my gaze lingering on his handsome face, keen to hear more.

"You were? As in joining the League?"

With a bob of his head, Colton smiles. While it's not wide and bright, it's not filled with the sadness that I expected. Of course, he could be inflating this story and exaggerating. As soon as I think it, I know it's not the case. Sure, we've still got a lot to share— the small and some huge stuff too—but he's a solid guy and doesn't need to add bullshit for Mav to like him, or for me to, for that matter.

From the time we've spent together, on the court, curled around each other when we can find the time, and in the countless phone conversations and texts, there's little doubt in my mind that I'm getting to know the man well.

Hell, these days, beyond my boy, my parents, and my best friend, Tony, I expect he knows more about me than anyone else does. Maybe not all my secrets or my pain yet, but enough for a real connection.

"Yeah. You ever heard of Montview Academy?"

Mav shakes his head at Colton's question, and I'm right there alongside him.

"It's a summer school—" An abrupt laugh and nose scrunch from Mav makes Colton pause before continuing. "One where college players who are on the right path to go pro play basketball for weeks with a team of coaches. Some are active League players too."

"That's so cool." Mav is quick to change his tune. "Dad, can I go next summer?"

"Did you not hear the 'college players' part?" His enthusiasm is freakin' magic. I hope he never loses it. Even if it's for a sport I'm a complete novice at.

"Oh, yeah. But I could when I'm at college?"

A huff of amusement spills out of me. "I'm sure if you work really hard in class and you show real talent on the court, you'd be in for a shot." It's not my job to step on the kid's dreams.

Wide-eyed, he stares at Colton. "It sounds amazing." His expression slips, brow furrowing with concern. "You said you were close to going pro, right? What happened?"

I part my lips to pull Mav up, more than aware not everyone is comfortable with being bombarded with questions.

Before I can intervene, Colton's lips tilt up a little. "Hurt myself pretty bad. Unfortunately it was a game-changer and stopped me from playing twenty hours of ball a week."

"Twenty hours?"

While Mav's stuck on that, I study Colton, my heart hurting for the guy. I know what it's like to have your dreams torn from you. To have the course of your life upended.

Colton's half shrug is a little too controlled.

Reaching out, I place my hand on his forearm, squeezing lightly. It's impossible not to offer him some comfort. More than that, I want to. Want to let him know I can tell that despite his brave face, it hurts.

He directs a sweet smile my way, and I want more than anything to lean in and place a kiss on his lips. My stare is hard, promise forced into my gaze. When his smile turns into a smirk, I know he understands.

"Here you go." Fiona reappears and places our drinks in front of us. "Are you ready to order?"

In truth, we've barely looked at the menu. I glance at Colton. "Do you need more time?"

With a shake of his head, he says, "If Mav recommends the burger with the works, I'll go with that."

I smile at him, at my kid's ecstatic grin, and make my order, knowing that it's almost time to share the hard stuff.

"NOTHING. DON'T BE RIDICULOUS." IT'S A GOOD thing Tony can't see the heat in my cheeks.

"And I call total bullshit." It's been almost a year since I saw my business partner, but it seems like it's not been long enough for him to miss hearing that something's shifted in my tone.

All I'd said was that life was good. Apparently before today's conversation about my annual trip to

Boston, I've been a miserable fucker. Something he's never called me out on.

"Is there a reason why you're denying it?"

I could act oblivious, but what would be the point. Why deny how much lighter, happier I've been feeling over the past few weeks? Isn't it amazing and a blessing to feel this way? "It's new."

There's a beat of silence that's long enough to have me looking at my phone's face to make sure we're still connected. We are, so I put it back to my ear.

"Holy shit, I was only half serious. But yeah… uhm… that's great, Will." Surprise seems to drive his words. "You know you can talk to me about this stuff, right?"

He's such a good guy who's always had my back. "Thanks. I'll be seeing you in less than a week. Maybe we'll talk about it then." I'm flying out on Thursday for a long weekend. It's time Tony and I have a sit-down about the company, the projections, significant hiring, and contracts.

Well, that takes up a small amount of time, in truth. We spend most of the time catching up, drinking beer, and reminiscing.

Beyond the official annual business meet up, the day-to-day is all his.

"Still, at least give me her name."

I smirk, kind of loving keeping Tony on his toes. He's rarely knocked off-balance. "Colton."

The pause has me glancing at the screen again.

"Oh, shit. Right." He clears his throat. "And aren't I a dick for assuming it was a woman." I can hear his mortification, but it's tinged with an unexpected tightness. Before I ask if everything is okay, a low chuckle filters through the line. "In my defense, I'm surprised more by the knowledge considering where you're living than anything else."

"Ha. Collier's Creek isn't quite the place it was twenty-five years ago, but I get it." When I told my parents at twelve years old that I liked a boy at school, they'd reacted with smiles and questions about who this boy was and followed up with hugs and love. There's no doubt I've always been seriously blessed with kick-ass parents.

But I hadn't really known anyone else much like me at the time.

But how things had changed in our small town.

Maybe it was the influx of new faces over the years. Perhaps it was that despite the size and location of our small community, the majority practiced what they preached: respect, compassion, and understanding.

Moving back home and seeing the difference in our town, the acceptance, is one of the reasons I knew it was the right place to return to and bring up Mav.

"So what's Mav think of Colton? They've met, right?"

"He's actually Mav's basketball coach. Thinks he's the best thing since Ryan Broadwater." Was that the only basketball player's name I knew before I met Colton? An absolute yes. And that was only because he was the first professional player to come out a couple or so years back.

As a bi man, I appreciated his bravery and the significance of the moment.

"Well, that's great."

"Yeah."

"What's with the slow *yeah*?"

I feel like a fool when I admit, "He doesn't actually know we're...." Fuck, how the hell do I finish that off? I suppose that's half the problem.

"I see. Because of Kelly?" Tony's voice is careful.

"No. Yes." I sigh. "Partly. More like I haven't told Colton about Kelly."

"Why the fuck not?" There's no heat behind his words, but he's surprised. He also sounds as confused as I am.

"Urgh. We've got such a good thing going. I don't want his pity stare."

Silence follows my words before the asshole, who I promise isn't as insensitive as he's coming across, bursts out into raucous laughter. "You're such a fucking dick. Man, stop overthinking this. Just fucking tell him. Accept his reaction, talk it through, and deal. I'm assuming this guy's important to you. That you see a future of some kind."

Once again his tone is slightly off, and I can't put my finger on exactly why that is.

"I do." The words are out before I can censor them. It's the first time I've admitted it aloud or even to myself.

"So stop being a chump, lay it all out there, and deal. Kelly was your world for a long time there. And I know you never want to hide her memory away."

I wince, feeling like a prize dick. Is that what I've been doing? "I really don't."

"Perfect. So invite him along this weekend. We have plenty of time between company bullshit for you to spend time with each other. You're staying in the fancy-as-fuck hotel. It'll give me the chance to get the measure of him."

I part my lips to say he's being ridiculous but slam them shut just as quickly. His idea has merit.

It'll give us a safe place to talk, and Tony's not wrong. I've booked a suite, and the bed really is nice and big.

"I'll see what I can do."

He's laughing loudly even as I say goodbye and call him an asshole.

With a newfound purpose, I stare at my phone, trying to contain my excitement. A weekend away with Colton sounds incredible. I just have no idea if it's possible. Can teachers just take a day off whenever they want? I don't expect so.

But I'm going to see if he's willing to make it happen.

CHAPTER NINE

COLTON

The unhinging of my jaw isn't my best look, but there's nothing I can do about it. "Uhm... what's happening right now?" I swivel to look at Will, who's caught between a wince and a smile and doesn't seem to know what emotion to settle on.

"When we get settled, there are a few things I need to tell you." A shifty look follows, and while I'm not nervous, 'cause, hello, private fucking jet, my brain is misfiring, struggling to compute.

"Okay." Even though a frown furrows my brow, I offer a smile.

Let's be real here—while I'm confused, this is all levels of exciting.

The silver jet is all sleek lines and polished panels. My heart races as I lead the way up the metal staircase, viscerally aware of Will at my heels.

"Welcome, Mr. Green."

Heat flushes my cheeks at the flight attendant who greets me. "Yes, hi, thanks." *The hell is going on?*

She smiles graciously and welcomes me on board with a hand gesture before smiling at Will. "Mr. Evans, so wonderful to see you again. Welcome aboard. If you'd like to settle down, I'll bring you refreshments. Champagne?"

I hover before sitting, peering over at Will. His smile is small as he says, "Hi, Melody. Champagne would be wonderful, please." He flicks his attention to me. "Is that okay or would you prefer—"

The shake of my head cuts him off. "No, champagne's great, thanks." I have a feeling it'll be the proper stuff too. Not fizzy wine masquerading as French Champagne. And I seriously need alcohol. Not that I think it'll help to ease my confusion, but I'm willing to give it a go.

Feeling a little at a loss about where to sit—not that there are many options with the limited seating and large space—I wait for Will to reach me. He pauses before me, concern entering his gaze. "You okay? Is this too much?"

At the genuine worry bleeding through his tone, I

reach for him, clasping his forearm, my thumb stroking his skin. "I'm fine," I reassure. "Just not quite sure where to sit, what to do," I admit. It's rare I feel out of my depth, but rather than wilting or even worrying, I'm more than okay to follow Will's lead.

From how he greeted Melody, it's clear this type of travel isn't new to him.

A warm smile tilts his lips, and he shifts his arm to take hold of my hand. "How about we sit here, together?" Will indicates two plush chairs that are side by side.

Sitting down, I take everything in.

The space is lavish. The seats are plush leather and quite possibly the most comfortable chairs I've ever sat on. While it's early morning and the sun appeared about thirty minutes ago, the overhead lighting is on and casts a soft glow. It's warm and welcoming.

I dart my gaze to the fresh flowers and the artwork, and I only just hold myself back from doing a double-take. It's elegant and screams wealth.

While I don't feel uncomfortable—how can I when I feel like I'm sitting on a cloud that's wrapping me in a hug—Melody appearing with a wide smile and a tray with two champagne flutes feels odd. A little awkward.

"Thanks," I manage, taking my drink. Will follows suit, and we're left to it again.

"You sure you're okay?"

I make eye contact and exhale. Jesus, it seems ridiculous, my reaction and how unsettled I feel.

"Are you feeling a little awkward?"

I snort, my shoulders relaxing. "Am I that easy to read?"

"Only to me."

Warmth flutters in my chest, liking his response a lot.

"I'll be fine." I roll my eyes, at myself more than anything. "It's a good thing I didn't go pro." My lips twitch.

"I suspect you would have soon got used to living the high life."

"You think?"

He shrugs, though his gaze remains intent. "Money can allow so many incredible doors to be opened and provide so many opportunities, but I think there's an important balance to establish so it doesn't rule your existence or destroy the possibility of living your best life." A small tilt of his head follows. "And I know only someone with money and who's privileged can say such a thing."

I nod and take a sip of my champagne. At the first caress of cool liquid on my tongue, I groan. "Holy shit." The words rush out of me. I take another sip, savoring the burst of bubbles.

Will's chuckles pull my attention to him. "Good?"

"So good." It really is. It's definitely the good stuff. Not that my uncultured self would be able to truly distinguish between the brands or anything.

"Feeling more relaxed?"

A smile forms quickly, and I angle to look at Will, appreciating his concern and his sweetness. "This is the best kind of awkward."

His laughter splits through any remaining discomfort I may have. I'm not even joking. If this is what awkward feels like, I'll take it.

I settle back into my plush seat and smile, listening intently as Melody comes out and speaks to us before introducing us to the pilot. Am I over-whelmed? Clutching my bubbles, I can't find the will to be. Instead, I'm happy to be here with Will, along for the ride.

That's not to say my curiosity isn't front and center.

Who am I kidding? Questions are bouncing

around my brain with such speed that I can't grab one fast enough to voice any of them. It's easier to ignore them all and focus on what I can see rather than what is actually happening here.

Before long, we take off. I stare out the window, relaxing even more. Four hours or so in this level of comfort isn't exactly a hardship.

When we're told it's safe to unbuckle, Melody returns with a snack and a top-up. She then leaves us to it, disappearing behind a privacy divider.

"Shall we head toward the back?"

"Sure." I stand and follow him into another area of the plane that has large couch-like seating within a slight curve. We settle down, angling toward each other. I take another sip of my champagne, not quite ready to let the bubbly goodness go.

"I imagine you have questions."

I do, but rather than firing them off, I say, "How about you just tell me what you want to share?"

Not a chance I'm putting pressure on him to divulge his secrets. I have several things I've yet to share. Some make me uncomfortable as hell. But I do intend to share more with him. Maybe what he has to tell me today will give me the confidence to do that.

I haven't shied away from how much I enjoy

spending time with him. Whether it's between the sheets, talking on the phone, or hanging out with Will and Mav, each second offers me a highlight to my day and is definitely something I look forward to.

"I met Tony in my second year at college," he starts. I listen intently, aware that Tony is his friend in Boston who we're going to see. "When we graduated from MIT"—my eyes round. *MIT? Holy shit*—"we went for it, took a small loan from his parents to help with start up, and officially opened our cyber-security firm."

Wide-eyed, I stare at him. "But you're a barista." Even as the words fall out, I know they sound ridiculous. All my earlier questions and confusion start to fall into place. Ones I had when we first met.

"I am a barista. Like I was at college, and for a few hours a day during the week, that's my job." A soft smile plays on his lips. I latch onto it. Not his lips, as that would be weird, but rather on the hum of quiet patience buzzing from him.

Putting down my glass, I bob my head, ready to hear more.

"From there, we finished working on new programming we'd started creating when at college together, finally having the time and cash coming in from the small accounts we were managing to secure. When we launched the new program four years after starting, it kind of took off." The shrug he shares is a little uncomfortable. A hint of pink touches his cheeks, and he rubs the back of his neck.

The whole time, his gaze doesn't waver from mine. He's waiting for a reaction. To be bombarded by questions, I imagine.

Realization trickles in, and I tug my gaze from his and glance around at the lavish plane. "Is this *your* jet?" There's a catch in my breath I can't control.

"The company's."

He's still watching me intently.

"*Your* company's?" I clarify.

"Well, it's a joint partnership, but yes. Fortress-Cyber owns it."

"O-kay," I say slowly. "This is a lot," I admit.

A fast head bob follows as he leans forward, tentatively reaching out for my hand. I don't like it at all, his hesitation.

I snag his hand, and I hold his palm, shooting him a smile. It forms easily, naturally. How can it not when he's being so ridiculously sweet. And his nerves? It's kind of flattering, to be honest.

On contact, his tentative smile stretches wide, and my heart bounces around.

Processing is going to take some time, but this is hardly a deal breaker. Questions, though—I have a million and one. The most important being, "Why did you move back to Collier's Creek?" *Give it all up?* remains unsaid.

There's no missing the sadness creeping into his face. My heart stumbles for very different reasons.

"You don't have to ans—"

"Kelly, my wife, died of breast cancer."

My breath whooshes out of me. Even if he can't say any more, it's enough. Understanding begins to form in my overloaded brain. Understanding why he would want to be close to his parents. Understanding why he would step away from his business so he can dedicate his energy to his son.

Sadness prickles my skin. My heart constricts. Jesus, it would be inappropriate, right, to climb onto his lap and hug him so damn tightly, I might make it difficult for him to breathe?

"I can't even imagine all you've been through," I settle on. At least we're still holding hands so I can squeeze his palm. "Does Mav get his stubbornness, which I've witnessed several times now, and his love of basketball from Kelly?"

A flash of something darts across Will's expression. It's there for but a moment. It's replaced by something even better. A wide smile and loud, abrupt laughter. It's from deep in his belly, by the sound of it. It morphs his face into an expression of happiness. I don't miss the sheen in his eyes, but his laughter has chased away whatever sadness was creeping into him.

"Holy shit," he manages between his laughter. He shakes his head, chuckling loudly, scooting even closer to me so our knees are touching. "He really does." Wonder fills his gaze as he looks at me with an emotion I have to react to.

I clamber onto his lap, not giving a flying fuck about the flight attendant who's hidden away or how many thousands of feet we are up in the air.

Straddling him, I smirk and peer down, loving the brightness beaming up at me. Will loops one arm around me, holding me close. His other hand settles on one of my ass cheeks.

I don't speak, waiting for him to continue. Waiting for him to share pieces of himself.

"When Mav doesn't want to do a chore, he gets this expression on his face that is all Kelly. I can practically see his brain ticking over, coming up with a counteroffer. A list of reasons why the chore should be overlooked and where his time would be more valuably spent."

Chortling, I dance my fingers through the hair at the back of his head. "What did Kelly do?"

"She was in HR. A recruiter. Not in FortressCyber, my company. But we had dealings quite early on after starting up. She could negotiate the hell out of a deal."

Compassion blooms deep in my stomach for all Will must feel and what he and his son have been through. "If she's anything like Mav, it's not hard to imagine how incredible she was."

A soft expression settles on his face, and he holds me even tighter. "Thank you. She really was."

This is all the talking for now.

With years of experience at reading my students, knowing when they're on the edge and when not to push, I'm sure Will is close. I lean down, place a gentle kiss on his mouth, and press my face against his neck while attempting to hug him.

The position's not exactly comfortable, and I'm too tall to do a good job of it, but the connection is important. And I'll take the sore neck if it offers Will any semblance of peace.

I'VE BEEN LEFT TO MY OWN DEVICES MOST OF THE afternoon, exploring Downtown Boston. It's been helpful, giving me time to try to process everything Will shared with me.

While he hasn't given me numbers, a company that he has equal shares in that has its own private jet screams wealth. And I'm talking more than Cassius wealth here. And I know my League-playing friend recently signed a cool eight-million-dollar contract and earns big bucks in advertising deals.

Cassius doesn't have a private jet.

Am I overwhelmed? A little. But every time I think of Will and how... shit, how "normal" he is, how down to earth... my frantic pulse calms. There's also Mav, who's a regular kid. And in my biased opinion, a freaking *amazing* kid. He's thoughtful and helpful. Sure, he's also ten and can be a grump and give his dad some grief, but there's no arrogance there.

No self-entitlement.

Does he know about his dad's wealth? Even as I think that, I dismiss it. Of course he does, but he's also spent half his life in Collier's Creek with a dad who works as a barista.

While we haven't talked about it, I suspect the reason why Will took on the job too. Pretty confident I'm correct—that he works because of Mav, to show him how important it is to work hard and have responsibilities, and I suspect to provide a semblance of community too—I can't help but wish we were meeting up in the hotel suite rather than being social.

He deserves all my attention tonight, and not even because of the fancy, easy trip to Boston. Or even the impressive suite in the five-star hotel.

No, Will deserves all my attention because he's edged his way into the spot of being the best person I know. A little bit of worshipping will go at least some of the way to show him how happy I am he came into my life—and allowed Mav to convince him to volunteer to help me coach.

Devouring him can happen in a few hours.

It's the promise of that I hold on tightly to as I relax my shoulders, straighten my shirt, and step into the bar Will asked me to meet him and Tony at. This was only after he'd tried to return to the hotel first so we could walk together. Sweet but completely unnecessary.

Despite being in a busy city all afternoon, the volume in the bar hits me in the face, taking me by surprise. You'd think my daily task of wrangling noisy teenagers and my basketball training sessions with rambunctious ten-year-olds would have prepared me.

Apparently not.

Boston, this bar, the buzz of the city are such a far cry from what I've grown to love about small-town living. I'm just relieved that through the pack of people who are laughing, talking intently, and whose gazes are roaming the place, I have height on my side.

Spotting Will easily just as his attention shifts to the entrance, I shoot him a warm smile.

How is it possible that I've missed him so much?

At home, we don't get to see each other every day of the week, but something shifted on our flight over. At the heart of that was Will sharing something so personal and painful. It's impossible not to feel the change gut deep.

And I am 100 percent here for it.

He stands as I approach, all smiles as his gaze eats me up. From that look alone, my pulse vibrates—maybe he's missed me too.

"Hey," I greet, going willingly into his space when he stretches out his arm, clasps my waist, and maneuvers me closer. It's possessive, and since I'm feeling all levels of needy, his display simply ramps up my desire and how quickly my heart pounds.

Rather than answer, he seals his mouth over mine. Right here in this busy bar.

I sigh into the gentle kiss, reciprocating the press and slide of his lips, but all too soon, I lose the connection when he pulls away just on the right side of the kiss being PG.

"I missed you today." The words wash over me, the sound of them vibrating against my neck since he said them close so he didn't need to shout.

Angling back to meet his eyes, what I find there has me swallowing hard. Undoubtedly he feels the change. Absolutely he's wishing we were wrapped up in each other in the fancy suite he procured for us.

It's not hard to throw heat into my eyes, my smile, letting him know I feel the same.

"Really, William. Stop hogging the poor man. Let him get a drink to cool him off, and maybe down one yourself to put out the fucking fire in your pants." Glee fills the words, and when Will angles away and shifts from before me, I'm met with bright blue eyes, a handsome face, and the biggest shit-eating grin I think has ever been sent my way.

The man stands, stretching out his hand for me to take. "I hope to fuck you're Colton. If not, that's all levels of awkward."

I huff out a laugh, heat touching my cheeks, and shake his hand. "Tony, I presume."

"One and the same." He indicates for me to take a seat. Considering how busy the place is, I imagine they had to fight off more than one person trying to drag it away while they waited for me.

"I got you a beer. That okay?" Will settles beside me, picks up the waiting beer, and places it before me.

"That's perfect, thanks." My soft smile is all his as a satisfied smirk plays on his lips. He scoots his chair even closer, his thigh pressing against mine. His strong hand then settles on my denim-clad leg.

On contact, I relax even more.

"So, Colton…."

Talk about being caught up in each other. Will and I jerk our gazes apart, finding a tight-smiled Tony, but the humor doesn't lighten his eyes like I'd expect.

"Tony," I manage, not holding back my chagrined smile.

"Behave," Will says from beside me, though his words are all for his friend.

"Me? I'm the epitome of social decorum and angelic compared to the two of you." A tight amusement tinges each word. Turning his attention to me,

Tony's intense blue eyes zero in. "Should I start by asking your intent—"

"No, you should fucking not," Will huffs out.

Despite Will's interruption, Tony doesn't look away from me. While the man's smiling, I kind of think he's serious about the question. Not a chance am I answering, though. Will, even in his amusement, doesn't want me to be dragged into Tony's inquisition.

That I can read Will's tone and intent enough to understand that sends a fresh thrill of contentment through me.

Tony's "Fine" follows a moment later.

Maybe he can read my resolve. Maybe he knows when not to push. Whatever the reason, I smile and pick up my beer.

"Will tells me you're a science teacher and you're brave enough to coach youth basketball."

With a head bob, I set down my beer, happier for the light "getting to know you" conversation. "For my sins, yeah. In all seriousness, I love it most days. And the basketball…. Young kids have their challenges. I'm used to coaching teams who are a little older, but it's good fun getting back to basics, and there's nothing like the feeling of being the first to spot raw talent."

It's a serious rush and a hell of a responsibility to home in on that talent so these novice players get the buzz and start to feel the passion for the game.

"And that's where you met Will, through Mav."

It's a statement, but I nod anyway. "That's right." Turning my head so I can see Will's face, I somehow manage to hold back the giddy sigh his warm smile tries to drag from me. In response to whatever he sees in my expression, he squeezes my thigh.

Looking back at Tony, I smile, saying, "And how about you guys?" It's time to turn the focus away from picking apart my relationship. "Did you have a successful day?" My attention drifts between the two of them as I speak.

"It was. Not the most exciting of days admittedly," Will answers.

"That's what you get when you're no longer part of the fun stuff." There's a tightness around his eyes despite the amusement in his voice.

"I've got all of the fun I need happening back home in Collier's Creek."

Tony's gaze narrows a fraction, his smile still in place but looking more forced.

Whatever is going on here is something I don't want to be a part of. The friction between them, I'm assuming, is business related, so nothing at all to do with me.

I part my lips to change the subject but stop short when Tony says, "I can see that."

The bite in his tone makes me do a double-take. There's a fierceness in his gaze that absolutely wasn't there before. The welcoming humor when we met just ten minutes ago is nowhere in sight.

I have no idea if this whiplash of emotions is normal for him or not, but from a quick glance at Will, he seems weary.

Fuck, I should have accepted Will's offer to head back to the hotel and trapped him in our suite instead.

"Don't start."

That's definitely exhaustion in Will's voice. Maybe they've been at odds all day.

"You asked for time. I gave it to you. Now you've got someone warming your bed, it's a done deal and the end of all we've worked toward for practically twenty fucking years." Ice cold, Tony's voice cuts through the air around us. While his voice isn't loud, more than a few heads turn in his direction.

"Enough."

I freeze at the hardness of the single word coming from Will. I've never seen him pissed before.

That tone alone could make a person cower. Add in the glint in his eyes, and it's like looking at a different person, enough so to make me catch my breath.

At the sound, Will's sharp gaze turns to me. It softens immediately, and something akin to regret appears on his expression.

"We can go," I offer, my tone gentle. I want to make it clear I'm here for him and none of his anger impacts me at all.

"Yeah, why don't you go and head off into the sunset with your little science teacher."

The fuck?

I turn my head so damn fast, if I wasn't sitting, I could have fallen. Somehow I don't flinch at the animosity in Tony's hard stare. It'll take more than an egotistical prick with a chip on his shoulder to truly get under my skin.

"Tony." Will is furious. And while whatever is going on here is really nothing to do with me, all I can see happening is anger and spite growing unless I intervene.

Between playing college basketball, dealing with my brother and his world of violence and chaos, and teaching angry teenagers, I'm hardwired to let the bullshit and aggravation roll on over me. None of that shit will stick to me. I settle my hand on Will's arm. His muscle is taut under my touch. I give him a light squeeze, and he relaxes a little.

"It's time for us to go." My attention is wholly on Tony. A flash of his gaze on my hand, on the way I'm holding on to Will, and realization hits me.

He's in love with Will.

Sure, there's more going on here from the sound of it, but the pain in his gaze, even though brief when it settled on my hand comforting Will, was there clear as day.

Did Will see it? Does he know?

"Tony." He lifts his gaze when I say his name. "Perhaps the two of you need to cool down before either of you say more that you'll regret and can't take back." With a steady voice, I continue, "Will and I may only be at the start of our relationship, but it's something special. Something I've never had before. I'm not prepared to let him go."

At the tightening of Tony's jaw, I hold back a sigh. Saying any more is likely a waste of my time.

So I don't.

Angling toward Will, whose gaze is completely on me, I don't resist the soft smile I shoot his way. How can I when he's looking at me like I matter?

"Let's go, baby." The endearment slips out, feeling right.

His eyes flash, and he nods, immediately standing. He takes my hand in his. After a squeeze and a slight tug, he then turns to Tony. I glance in the other direction, giving them the tiniest semblance of privacy. "Only call tomorrow if you've pulled your head out of your ass."

Fucking hell. I clamp my jaw tight and am so pleased I'm looking away. The bubble of laughter at the frustration and snark in Will's words lodge in my throat.

Locking myself down from snickering inappropriately, I lead him away. I have no idea how Will is feeling, but my laughter is so far from appropriate considering the blow up between him and his business partner.

With the breeze on my skin, I lose the desire to laugh. "I think we should walk." The cooling evening air will help blow away the negativity clinging to us from that exchange.

At Will's soft "Okay," I know it's the right thing to do. We need to have a conversation after all that's transpired, but for now, I offer him my quiet support as we stroll hand in hand back to the hotel.

CHAPTER TEN

WILL

Unable to settle on a single emotion, I fight not to explode. If not that, then curl in on myself. Neither are what I want to do.

Our walk back to the hotel was silent, Colton knowing what I needed without me having to say a word. But now, freshly showered, every part of me cleansed and practically sparkly, I need Colton to drive away the emotions I can't get a handle on.

On the bed in his black boxers, ankles crossed, gaze on the sports channel playing quietly on the TV, Colton looks delectable. Every single inch of him. As soon as I open the bathroom door fully, his focus turns to me.

Eyebrows launching up, Colton rakes his wide

eyes over me, his gaze heating and filling with hunger.

Being naked tends to cause that reaction. My cock likes it a lot, twitching and hardening under his scrutiny. It's not just my dick, though. With my pulse increasing, my heart pummeling my rib cage, I'm certain this is both what I want and what I need.

As I draw closer to the bed, he sits up, placing one hand behind himself to lean on as he stretches out the other hand to me. "Come here, baby."

There's that word again. The tenderness wraps around me, and my heart stutters. I go willingly, eagerly, kneeling onto the bed and making my way on my knees until I'm before him.

He doesn't ask if I'm okay. Doesn't ask me what the fuck happened between me and the man I consider my best friend. That Colton doesn't ask those things solidifies how well he knows me.

It hasn't been long in the grand scheme of my life, but rather than terrifying me, I latch on to the wonder of our connection and having this chemistry with him after less than a couple of months.

Swallowing down the nerves as I stare into his deep-brown eyes, I ask for what I need, "I want you. I want to be under you."

The barest of seconds pass before he bobs his

head, but I see something lurking beyond the surface of his lust. Not wanting him to hold back, I say, "If you want me too." While I'm sure he does, it doesn't stop anxiety from fizzing in my chest.

"Of course I want you," he says immediately, easing the worry clenching my heart. "So fucking much. I just want to make sure you want this because it's me… it's *us* and not just because you want to escape and get lost."

Fuck. Tears form in my eyes, and I hate them. Hate how the evening ended up. My heart is wrecked from Tony sending my world completely spinning during our earlier meeting and the shit-show in the bar.

"Hey." Colton reaches for me, and I go willingly, falling into his open arms and then with him onto the bed, where we settle together. "Let's just stay here like this for a while."

This man is so ridiculously perfect that my lips attempt to lift into a smile. They can't quite manage it, so instead, I press a kiss to his neck where my face is buried. I tighten my hold on him, one leg over his, my arms wrapped around him as he cradles me in a warm hug.

My thoughts begin to calm, my emotions settling. For the first time since I sat down with Tony and sensed, then knew, something was off, I can finally breathe again. A deep inhale and exhale, and I snuggle even further against Colton.

"Thank you for earlier," I mumble after a few minutes of quiet.

"I didn't do anything." A press of his lips to my head punctuates his words.

"You did. You stopped that situation from spiraling and got me out of there without me exploding or knocking some sense into him."

Loosening his grip, Colton angles away a little. I look up as he does so, and we make eye contact. He peers back at me with concern. "I'm not sure if me being here made things worse for you, but I kind of suspect they did."

I wince and don't refute his words.

"But I'm glad I'm here."

"You are?"

The smallest of breathy chuckles escapes him. "You're naked in my arms. We have a kick-ass suite and alone time." A shrug follows. "So yeah, this moment right here, is the start of so many fantasies coming to life."

My flagging dick twitches, earning me a salacious smirk. "My fantasies too."

Colton trails his fingers up my back until they

reach my neck. As he strokes his thumb across my cheek, his gaze searches mine. "Never doubt how much I want you. I need to be sure you want to for the right reasons." Pink spreads across his cheeks, sparking my curiosity and keeping me quiet. "It sounds ridiculous, as it's sex."

I understand what he's getting at. We've had discussions over the past few weeks. He's told me about his past relationship years ago, just like he also told me about a couple of regular hookups before moving to Collier's Creek.

Sex didn't have to be a big deal. I lived with that mindset at college and before I met Kelly. And with Colton, fuck if I felt like actual intercourse was huge. Especially considering I told him I wanted to be under him.

"I get it," I finally answer. "It means something between us." The words he fired off at Tony rush to the surface. "What you said at the bar…." I trail off, not sure how to finish.

"I meant them."

"I know." That's not something I ever doubted. Thinking about his words, my heart chooses what I need to say for me. "I never want to let you go either."

A spark. A glow that hits my chest, spiking my pulse before it races over my skin.

I don't need grounding. I want us to soar together, for the arc of awareness between us to build into something blinding. Something permanent.

I heard his worry. Listened to his heart. Having pulled both inside, I am so ready for more. I crave his closeness, his touch, so deep that I can lose myself in the warmth of his embrace, finding solace in his desire to never let me go.

Colton leans in, his lips brushing against mine with a soft whisper of a kiss.

"I want this with you." The words land between us as I lean back, my gaze fixed on him, taking in every emotion he willingly lets me see. His captivating deep-oak eyes lock with mine, dilated pupils reflecting his desire, his lips slightly parting.

Not wanting him to pull away, I draw him close. Craving more. I press my mouth against his, our lips moving in a harmonious dance, our tongues seeking entry, and I kiss him with all the lust and longing that's been enveloping us since the day we met.

I grasp his hip, pulling him closer, yearning for more contact. I don't relent as our mouths fuse together, moving in perfect synchrony.

Nothing else exists except the taste, the touch, and the sensation of Colton. I surrender to the moment, to him, relishing the quietening of my mind, the certainty of my feelings for him. The rightness of us being together here in this moment.

The shift of his hand to the back of my head, the slight grip on my strands, shoots shivers of pleasure rippling through me. It's been so long since I felt this way, since I experienced the raw passion of a first time. Sure, we've been together, but this feels different.

Is different.

I've never had a man inside me before. Knowing it's going to be Colton, and hoping, wishing, praying that he will be the only one, carries me through any whispers of worry I may have.

There's no space for overthinking. No fear. Not when everything with Colton feels so incredible.

A groan escapes him as his strong hand settles on my ass. With flexing, agile fingers, he hauls me closer. There's fabric in the way.

Wanting to feel Colton completely, I force myself away.

"Hey!"

I grin at how disgruntled he sounds, at the narrowing of his eyes at the small distance between us. When I slide my hands to his boxers, the glint in his eyes returns, and he hastily lifts to help me remove the black material.

"Lube's on the cabinet," he says, his voice tight with need.

I bob my head, having already spotted it. I also saw the condoms. I reach for the lube and place it on the mattress so it's within reaching distance. I grab a condom and hold it up between us.

"I know we talked about our health a while back, but I wanted you to have options."

And fuck if his response isn't perfect. So perfect, in fact, I need more of his kisses and definitely his naked skin against mine.

Throwing the unopened packet to the side, I sweep in for a kiss, immediately sighing into the connection.

As he entwines his tongue with mine, a surge of awareness shoots through every fiber of my being. My head spins, consumed by the sensations of him being everything I need. I wrap my arms around him, losing myself in the moment. In the kiss. At the flick of his tongue. His roaming hands. His hard cock rubbing against mine.

Catching Colton's soft grunt as our bodies press together fully, I refuse to let up.

And then I gasp as a single finger enters me. Coated in slick, it slides in effortlessly. My open-mouthed gasp mingles with a smile. "Yes," I manage, my voice barely above a breath. "Feels so good."

Colton is slow, attentive, his focus solely on me.

Once I've loosened and my eyes are already rolling to the back of my head, two, then three fingers join the first. Spots already dance before my eyes as I ride his digits. I can't even kiss him, too focused on the bliss of being stretched.

But I need his cock buried deep inside me. Am desperate to feel whole. To feel like I'm really his and that we're together in this.

A grunt escapes Colton when I take hold of his arousal. He's all heat and velvet, wrapping a hardness I know I'm going to feel for days. A deep groan follows, his breath catching when I squeeze gently.

"I'm ready. So fucking ready." Longing carries my words.

In a swift motion, he withdraws his fingers and manhandles me onto my back. My chuckle is cut off as he coats his length with slickness, then positions himself at my entrance. There's an intensity in his gaze I've never seen before. Not once. Not even with the multiple orgasms we've shared.

My lips part, ready to utter the words to encourage him to sink inside me, but before I can speak, he thrusts into me with a single confident stroke.

A silent cry escapes as ecstasy surges through me. Words become unnecessary as I hold my breath and surrender to Colton. With each forceful thrust, he fills me completely. But it's his eyes and the gentle touch of his fingers, so at odds with his strong, determined thrusts, that keep me hovering on the edge of falling.

His sweat-drenched brow glistens. I'm desperate to follow the path with my tongue, but all I can do is hold on tight and let him lead.

"You feel so incredible." Desire laces his words.

Unable to speak, I bob my head, lips still parted with the intensity of being filled by him.

In response, he dips down and captures my mouth, breathing against my lips before he kisses across my cheek and down to my neck. "You're amazing. Fuck."

Holding on to Colton even tighter, I move against him, trying to ensure every single piece of him is buried inside me. I'm desperate. Clingy. Hell, I feel like I'm having an out-of-body experience. With my mind close to whiting out, my balls pulling up tight, and my heart close to bursting, I'm struggling to breathe.

I don't want this to ever end. Don't want Colton to ever let go.

Pleasure burns under my skin. A deep ache forms with an intensity that hovers between bliss and torture. This right here is everything I didn't realize I needed.

Colton finds my mouth, capturing my lips in a searing kiss, leaving an indelible imprint of his taste on my memory. Just as I lean into him, ready to devour his mouth, he pulls away, going to his knees as he tugs me onto his thighs.

A groan escapes as our gazes meet and the angle changes. My eyelids close on their own volition, overwhelmed by the depth and new position.

"Okay?"

"Yeah," I manage, snapping my eyes open. "Amazing."

A tender smile forms on his kiss-swollen lips, and here, in this moment, I surrender completely. He can lead me wherever the hell he wants, and I'll go willingly.

Knowing I'm being ridiculous, a bubble of hysteria forms in my chest,.

"What?"

Realizing I'm smiling, I huff out a quiet, breathy laugh. A groan follows when he pushes deep and stays there a beat before pulling out. No fucking way can I tell him where my thoughts went. I may as well just be shouting three words at him and be done with it.

It's been years since I've been in this position, and I'm out of practice, but telling someone the depth of your emotions when balls deep is a no-no. Even I know that.

But he's waiting.

Colton hasn't stopped thrusting, but he's slowed down. His control is impressive, which is something to file to memory and explore another time. But not now. Not when I want to feel his cum buried inside me. Not when I want my release to paint his stomach.

"I'm just so fucking happy."

It's the only truth I can offer right now.

A flicker of emotion flames in his gaze, his smile tender, but it's quickly replaced with lust-fueled determination. Colton takes hold of my thighs and locks them in his grip, laying me open.

I'm at his mercy, and I love it.

He moves within me, each stroke hitting a depth that ignites stars behind my now-closed eyelids. My arousal pulses, balls tingling once again. I take myself in hand.

The groan tearing out of Colton when I do so has my eyes opening and widening. His attention is on my hand and how I'm jerking myself.

The intensity threatens to overwhelm me. From his gaze, the emotion I see there, and the feel of my dick in my palm combined, I'm close to the edge. Ready to tumble over and fall into oblivion.

Colton has other ideas.

He leans forward, gently clasps my cheek, and presses his lips to mine. Not expecting the tenderness, the kiss catches my breath. Sweet slides, gentle strokes, and a multitude of unspoken whispers and promises. Each sweep of his mouth and exploration of our tongues brings me closer to the precipice, threatening to send me spiraling into an abyss of ecstasy.

My hand falters as heat ignites, and finally, I detonate. I come with abandon. His mouth muffles my cries as I shudder through my release.

Breaking the kiss, Colton fixes his gaze on me. One thrust. Two. And then he groans, his lips parting and glistening, before I lose sight of him as he buries his face against my neck. I hold on tight, encouraging him to give me his weight. I can't make out his mumbled words beneath the thundering pulse in my ears.

With his breaths becoming more controlled, he holds me tightly before easing out of me. A groan slips past my lips, the feeling unlike any I've experienced.

"Let me just get a cloth to—"

"Not yet." I tug him down and maneuver so we're on our sides and face to face. I open my tired eyes, a lazy, content curve lifting my lips. Colton's already smiling softly at me, aiming a tenderness my way I'm beginning to recognize and associate with how he feels about me.

No more words are needed as I press against him, placing a tender kiss on his neck as he envelops me in his embrace. He's giving me this time, and I'm grateful.

Today has been a head fuck—for him especially, considering all he's learned—but he's taking it all in his stride and isn't holding back.

Snuggling close together in the quiet room, I exhale, silently thanking Colton for being the incredible man he is. For the first time in years, my mind's at peace, my body's sore yet so wonderfully alive, and my heart… yeah, it's very close to whispering those three words.

CHAPTER ELEVEN

COLTON

"I WANT TO TALK ABOUT YESTERDAY."

I still my hand before continuing to gently stroke Will's arm. "Okay."

"I'm sorry for the way Tony behaved."

Stopping again, I angle to see his face. "Don't apologize for other people's behavior." It's something I've discovered the hard way after countless years of doing so for my brother. "You're not responsible for Tony's actions."

"I know." A heavy sigh follows. "But I should have at least canceled after-work drinks. I just didn't think."

Still running my fingers over his skin, I wait patiently for him to continue.

"Tony and I clicked back in college. He became

my best friend. But I suppose you could say he's always been a bit protective of me."

That'll be because the guy's madly in love with you, I think.

"When I met Kelly a couple years out of college, Tony and I were already in business together, working hard at building our company, our software. He wasn't a fan of Kelly at first, but he eventually got over himself and stopped being an asshole. By the time Mav was born, we were all close. Tony dotes on Mav and is his uncle in all but blood."

"And yesterday," I can't help but ask, "has that sort of thing happened before?"

Will shuffles a little, moves so we can talk face to face. "Nothing like that." With his nose and brow scrunching, he frowns. "When I stepped away from the company five years ago, I discussed selling my shares. Tony would have none of it, so we agreed I'd become a silent partner. We meet once a year in an official capacity to go through relevant details, and he'll only reach out to me about the company if there's something in the works that he thinks needs my attention."

Understanding hits me. "He thought you'd go back." My gut clenches at the thought.

"Yeah." A humorless snort chases his word. "I sort

of suspected that's what he was hoping for, but yesterday he came out and said as much."

"And is that something you've always planned to do or would consider?" I ask carefully, pushing curiosity into my tone rather than the hint of worry at the possibility of Will moving away.

After a beat, during which I'm not sure if he's searching for my reaction or he's deep inside his own head, he answers, "Maybe." Another sigh. "I suppose when I left and he made the offer for me to remain as joint partner, it took the pressure off and let me hold on to a part of my old life. A bit of a life-line so that once I reached the point of knowing I could go this alone, be a single dad, live without Kelly, Mav and I could move back to Boston and pick up where we left off if I wanted to."

It made sense, but it had been five years. At least half of Mav's life was in Collier's Creek. From the time I've spent with the ten-year-old, I can honestly say he's happy and settled and definitely at home. Plus he spends a lot of time with his grandparents.

What does that mean for Will?

"Yesterday," he continues while my head and heart buzz with worry at losing Will when we're at the start of something amazing, "Tony asked me outright when I'd be returning." He shakes his head, hurt entering his gaze. "We had an argument when I told him I'd never agreed to that. Not once. He said I'd been leaving him hanging, dangling a carrot or some shit for him, making him believe I'd return to my old life, to him."

He peers at me with genuine confusion. Does he really not understand? Has he never seen Tony's real motivations? The depth of his feelings?

"By the end of our meeting, we'd calmed everything down. I explained how happy and settled Mav is. How our lives were coming together. By the time we left to meet you, he was laughing and joking. Sure, I was a bit thrown by his outburst, but there's also a big deal on the table with a huge company, which I know he's stressed about. I even offered to consult remotely once a month if it'll help take the pressure off. I finally feel able to do that now."

"And then over drinks he, what, lost his shit? Dragged me into his frustration with you? Why do you think that is?" I want him to draw the conclusion himself, but maybe he's just too close and can't see beyond his friendship.

Regret morphs Will's expression. "He was so out of line. I've never seen him behave that way ever before. I know you don't want to hear it, but I am so sorry, Colton. That's not the friend I know." He shakes his head. "I don't know what came over him."

What I want to do is rub a hand over my face, maybe give Will a shake too. Sure, I could be wrong here, but gut deep, I know I'm not.

"Maybe you need to ask Tony directly about yesterday and the real reason he blew up and attacked the both of us."

With his eyebrows pinched together, Will looks adorably, frustratingly clueless.

"Perhaps ask him what he thinks his future looks like?"

"What, as in the company? Us expanding?"

Holy fuck. I roll onto my back and release a weary groan. Relenting, I rub a hand over my face.

"What are you thinking?"

Removing my hand, I peer at him. "For a smart man, Will, how can you not see what's going on here?" I shoot my eyebrows high and pointedly stare at him.

And there it is. It takes a few heartbeats, but real-ization hits. Wide-eyed, he shakes his head. "That's not— That can't be— He's never—"

"Uh-huh. Maybe take some time to unpack that a little and see what you settle on." Poor guy looks ready to have a damn heart attack. Sympathy has me reaching for him. "Why don't you grab a shower? Give yourself some time to process. I'll order some breakfast."

Will's nod appears to be on autopilot, and while it takes a few moments for him to move, he eventually does so. As I watch him walk into the bathroom, my stomach twists, hoping I did the right thing.

Tony and Will have a long history. They love each other. Even if Will's feelings of love aren't romantic, now that I've planted that seed in his head, will he start to reconsider how he feels? Fuck, what if he realizes there's something else in his emotions, in how he feels for his best friend?

If that's the case, it's likely he'll want to see if there's the possibility of something more between them, right? I've read a romance book a time or two over the years, seen plenty of movies with the best-friend trope. I know how this plays out in fiction.

Holy shit. What if I've just opened the floodgates and thrown them together?

If I have, will I let it play out and give Will the chance to explore, or will I fight for the man and his son, knowing both have already stolen a piece of my heart?

I bury my face in the pillow, catching Will's scent and inhaling deeply. The memory of being buried in

Will yesterday blankets me, wraps me up tightly, and refuses to loosen its hold.

Yesterday was more than sex. More than a hot fuck. It meant something.

How can I possibly let that go? And can I if Will asks me to?

Fuck my life and my big mouth.

Pancakes. I need to order a giant stack of pancakes and a mountain of coffee. Whether they'll be fuel for a fight or allow me to disappear into comfort, time will tell.

AFTER A QUIET BREAKFAST WITH WILL SPENT TALKING about our morning plans and not mentioning at all our earlier discussion, we head to Quincy Market. Originally the plan was for Will to meet with Tony for the whole day, but apparently that's not happening.

While I think they need to talk, that Will's not rushing to Tony and is spending the day with me helps me breathe a little easier.

The tightness in my gut is still there, yanking and growing when I least expect it, but as we explore the market hand in hand, I grasp on to the knowledge that he's with me.

The market's alive and bustling with energy. I did a little reading before getting here, so I know the market is rich in history. It's also busy as hell. A pang of longing for my new town takes me by surprise. While Collier's Creek is such a small place and not at all what I'm used to, I'm happy there, comfortable.

Sure, that's because of the quaintness of the town, but it's also because of the people. While I'm still far from a local, I'm getting there. Someone always says hello in the street or at the grocery store. At first, I'd been a little freaked, worried about the impact of an "everyone knows everyone" place, but now, the warmth of the local faces and the ease with which I'm settling in makes Collier's feel very much like home and the place where I can see my future.

I just hope it stays that way.

My brother dragging me into his bullshit years back was enough to have me anxious about trusting anyone. Hell, if you can't trust family, who can you trust? Ha. That mantra flew out the window of a stolen car, got stained with a shit ton of drugs, and was ruined without repair when the police called me in for questioning—and then later as a witness.

Lexington, a place not too dissimilar to Collier's Creek, had once been a place I'd called home. Until I was encouraged to hand in my notice—despite no charges being pressed against me and the fact that I was completely innocent. With my landlord giving me notice, too, parents refusing to let their kids attend practice, and my principal being a weak asshole, it hadn't been hard to run.

I don't want that to happen again. If it does, I'm not sure how long I can keep taking the knock-downs. At some point, getting back up and starting again is going to prove to be too much.

With my gaze on Will, I wait at a small table. He's fetching us Boston cream pies. Pancakes still sit heavily in my stomach, but sugar-loaded cake won't hurt. I need every bit of sweetness I can get right now.

While we've chatted and smiled as we've explored the stalls, there's a tension between us I don't like. If Will wants to talk to me about his thoughts, he has every opportunity. I'm respecting his silence, but fuck if it isn't hard.

In all honestly, this whole thing sucks. Am I a dick for sharing my observations with Will? Unfortunately, I think the answer is a resolute yes.

If I'd kept my thoughts to myself, this morning would have likely started with more orgasms and the two of us drifting happily around the markets. So far, every step has felt like I'm dragging my feet through wet concrete.

Will tugs out his phone as he's waiting in line. Eyebrows dipping, he reads and scrolls. His lips twist before he huffs out a breath. While I can't see or hear a thing, he's broadcasting his frustration loud and clear.

It has to be Tony.

And then his fingers are flying across the screen. There's a pause before he frowns again, and then he's typing. Nausea swirls my stomach with each second that passes by.

I encouraged him to talk to Tony so they could clear the air. Is there a part of me that regrets that? Maybe a little. Being a grown-up sucks, but being a stupid responsible adult also means dealing with the hard stuff. That includes trusting Will to navigate through this.

Will's head jerks up, and he looks at the server. It's finally his turn. After pocketing his phone, he hands over some cash and turns, his gaze connecting with mine.

Thank fuck his smile is immediate. It goes a long way to settling my uncertainty.

"For you," Will says once he reaches my side. As he places my cake on the table, he leans in and dots a kiss on my mouth. I smile as he pulls away, liking his open affection a lot.

"Thanks." I eyeball the cake. "It really isn't a pie, huh?"

He chuckles and sits opposite me. "Most definitely not a pie. It's delicious, though."

"It looks it." It also tastes divine. I hum at the flavor of the vanilla cream, appreciating the smooth texture and the way it melts on my tongue.

"Carry on and I'm going to get jealous of the cake." Humor teases his words, and his eyes flash with heat.

I smirk, licking my fork in a way that's practically indecent considering we're in public. But I need this lightness. We both do after yesterday and the heaviness of our morning.

"Fuck." His tone turns gruff. "Maybe I should be jealous of the fork instead."

"Or—" I quirk my eyebrow and lean in a little, lowering my voice. "—we could take this Boston cream pie back to the hotel, and we won't need forks."

Lust-filled eyes peer at me, but the expression disappears as he swallows. Something new appears instead. Guilt.

"What is it?"

"Tony texted, asked to meet me."

Hurt tries to needle its way inside me, but I push it away. The emotion has no place here. Or at least that's what I try to convince myself. "Okay. You do need to talk things through." I exhale and shake off my fear and the tinge of jealousy trying to take root in my chest. I reach out and take his hand. "He's your best friend. You owe it to each other to talk this out. You also have a whole company to consider."

There's so much more I want to say, but my couple of months of knowing Will is nothing compared to the twenty years of Will and Tony knowing each other. It's a hard reality to swallow.

"Thank you for understanding." As Will swipes his thumb over my skin, a gentle smile appears on his lips. "I'll meet up with Tony, get this talked out and settled, and then how about we head out for a nice meal tonight? Let me wine and dine you?"

The wings beneath my rib cage flutter to life. This is his way of reassuring me, and I appreciate it. But that being said, I don't need to be wined and dined. I don't need an expensive restaurant where I won't be able to smother him in affection. "The hotel dine-in menu looked pretty nice to me. That way we can stay naked and enjoy dessert immediately after."

A broad smile stretches over his lips. "I like your plan much better."

"Thought you might." I follow up with a wink and take another bite of cake.

"I said I'd meet Tony soon. I figured we could get this out of the way."

I bob my head. "I'm good here. I can carry on exploring and find my way back. Just call me when you're done." Each word tastes bitter. I hate this, but I'm really trying to do the right thing and be the better man here.

It's true. Adulting really does blow.

CHAPTER TWELVE

WILL

It's impossible to not hear Colton's words in my head. What he not so subtly hinted at.

But every time I try to bring it up with Tony, I can't.

As he says, "The Carlisle account is my biggest concern," rather than paying attention to Tony, I'm analyzing every conversation we've ever had. Every touch and laugh we've shared. His reaction to Kelly… to Colton. How he behaved during my self-discovery stage at college when I slept my way through so many men and women that I'd need more than one pair of hands to count.

"…with the growth and expansion…"

Did Tony really disappear into his shell, effectively giving me the cold shoulder whenever I hooked up at college? A vague memory of him doing so itches at me. Was it with men and women or…. The more I consider it, the more clarity I'm getting.

"…we should be okay, though, now that…"

Men. It was definitely whenever I hooked up with a guy. Though, he was an asshat to Kelly, but only when he realized she was more than a casual hook-up. I rack my brain for more, struggling to make sense of everything.

"…what do you think?"

The words register as a question. I'm already looking at Tony, but my gaze snaps to his. What the hell was he talking about? "Drop me the link to the account. Give me some time to take a proper look." I don't blink as I wait to see if that's a passable answer.

He bobs his head and clicks a few buttons on his laptop. "Done."

"Thanks." It feels like I'm working on autopilot, navigating through the unknown.

Beyond a shadow of a doubt, I thought Tony had my back, and while it's not necessarily that I don't think that anymore, if he feels more for me, has been harboring his desire for more from me for potentially years, how can I trust our relationship?

"Are you sure you're okay?"

Once again my attention snaps to him, and we

make eye contact. Sadness seems to shroud him, and every time I see the emotion pulsing off him, it digs deep and hurts.

Before I can respond, he says, "I really am sorry." Pleading eyes implore me to believe him. He spent the first thirty minutes after we met up apologizing profusely for his behavior to me and to Colton. He gave reasons that included lack of sleep, stress over the new development, and a large account. I'd apologized if I'd let him down, while making it clear that Mav and I were building a good life for ourselves in Collier's Creek.

He nodded, said he understood.

We'd hugged it out and even cracked open beers, trying to wipe away the previous day.

But what remains is uncertainty. And I have no idea how to handle it.

"Perhaps we should take a break?" It's probably for the best. If we can relax a little, get back to how things were, we'll soon find our way.

"Well, we have worked through lunch."

My rumbling stomach answers, just loud enough to pull a laugh from us both.

Standing, Tony collects his phone from his desk while I stretch and head over to the comfy seating tucked away in the corner of his large office.

He follows me with fresh beers and his phone. "What sounds good?"

"I'd kill for noodle soup from Gene's."

"God, Gene's. I haven't ordered from there in ages." He bobs his head and gets to work on his phone. "You want a lamb flatbread as well?"

Since I'm salivating at the thought, I quickly nod. "Hell yes. You know me so well."

The sadness is back, pushing down at me, but in another blink, it's gone. Instead, Tony's smirking. "Damn straight I do, asshole. And don't you forget it."

"Do you remember this one?"

Tony is wasted. I'd been on my way there, too, about an hour and a half ago, but, realizing the time and recalling I had hot plans this evening, I cut myself off. For the last ninety minutes, I've been glugging water and trying to get Tony to do the same.

In my defense, I persuaded him to down two glasses before he'd caught on to my sobering-up plan. Tony is a stubborn ass at the best of times. Pour alcohol down his throat and his stubbornness grows legs. He may as well have a PhD in the damn thing.

A track from Death Cab For Cutie blares from the speakers around his office.

"I remember you going through an emo stage," I tease, laughing loudly when he flips me off—with the wrong finger. Yeah, he's that drunk. While he's distracted looking at his fingers and swaying on his feet, I turn the volume down a couple of notches and glance at my phone.

Colton is on his way. Not a chance am I going to be able to get Tony out of here and home to bed without some added muscle. Colton's going to message me as soon as he reaches the building so I can let him in.

My buzz has officially disappeared, and while I'm chuckling along with Tony, that he's this wasted isn't good. I can count on one hand the number of times he's been drunk in front of me. Perhaps that sounds odd, since he's the same age as me, but Tony's a bit of a control freak and doesn't like losing his inhibitions.

The last time we were drunk together was a week after Kelly died. Mav was with my parents, and while Tony resisted drinking, wanting to take care of me, he'd folded and drank right alongside me until the sun came up.

His support with everything, especially during Kelly's illness and when I lost her, meant so much. I'm not sure if I could have handled life without him. It's this reason that's made me so worried all day about broaching the possibility of him feeling more for me.

What if he says he does? What if he says he loves me and has done so for twenty years?

Selfishly, I don't want to deal with that. Am I a coward for not wanting to destroy our friendship? Maybe. But what good can it do?

I love Tony. He's the brother that I never had. He's my best friend, a part of my family. I don't want to imagine my life without him being such an important part of it. If he *does* want more with me, and it's out in the open, how do we possibly move on from that?

But fuck, maybe we need to air this shit out.

If he's waiting for me, for a chance for us to be together…. The thought tightens my chest. Tony deserves happiness and love. Can he find that if he's hung up on me? Is that why he's a perpetual bachelor?

The beep of a message alert has me jumping. It's Colton.

A quick glance shows me Tony's now included the study of his fingers in his weird dance as Death Cab For Cutie track keeps playing. Or hell, maybe it's a different song. They all sound the same to me.

"I'll be back," I call out, not wanting him to realize I've gone and start hunting for me.

There's likely still some staff around on the floor below, but his assistant has long gone home. The last thing Tony needs is to go wandering and have one of our employees run into him.

Tony gives a lazy smile in acknowledgment, and I slip away, heading toward the private elevator.

It doesn't take long to reach the ground floor or the main foyer. Colton's chatting to Franklin, one of the three evening security guards. They both look my way as I head toward them. "Thanks, Franklin."

"No problem, Mr. Evans. We were just talking basketball."

"Why doesn't that surprise me." I throw the man a warm smile. He's been working for the company for close to twelve years. "We're going to go up to collect Tony and head straight down to the basement. Can you ask his driver to meet us there in ten minutes, please?"

"Of course, Mr. Evans. I'll do that right away." He turns to Colton and says goodbye, giving me the chance to look my fill of the man who makes my heart beat as fast as his long strides eat up the distance between us.

While he's smiling, he doesn't hide his concern. The plan was for me to be back at the hotel at least an hour ago. How lucky I am that he's being so understanding doesn't pass me by.

"You okay?" He reaches for me, his hand landing on my forearm and squeezing.

I have no reservations, so I haul him close, pressing my mouth to his. The contact is brief but enough to loosen the knot in my chest. When I pull away, I press my face against his neck and inhale. Okay, I may not be as sober as I thought, but compared to Tony, who has liquor oozing out of his pores, I'm as dry as the Sahara Desert during a drought.

"I am now," I finally say, aware I'm just standing here, inhaling him like he's a delicious treat.

His low chuckle is melodic and one of my favorite sounds. I tell him as much.

He laughs again, squeezes me tightly, then steps out of my embrace. The smile he shoots me is bright.

There's less worry evident than a few moments ago. "So, this is you 'sober,' huh?"

The air quotes he includes have me narrowing my gaze, feigning indignance. "I haven't had a drink in over ninety minutes."

"Have you been keeping time?"

"No." I so had. I stopped when I first messaged Colton and have been keeping a close eye on how long I had to wait until I saw him.

"Uh-huh. And you said Tony's wasted?"

"Yeah." I nod, trying to make it a normal, regular type of nod, though it feels like my chin's almost touching my chest.

"Oh, boy." He glances around and pauses at the elevator. "Is this our ride?"

"It sure is." Hand in hand, we head to the elevator. I use my keycard to open the door and send us on our way to where I hope Tony's still happily dancing. It's funny, I felt virtually sober before I headed downstairs. Either it seemed that way because Tony's in such bad shape or being around Colton is intoxicating.

What I do know is, I need to untangle myself from Colton by the time the elevator stops. Tony's been chilled out and merry since drinking his weight in whiskey, but what I don't want is my loving up on my boyfriend to set him off.

"I just called you my boyfriend in my head." I tilt away from where I'm wrapped around Colton and peer up at him. "Is that okay? You feel like my boyfriend, and last night…" Just the memory of how we connected is difficult to grasp. It was everything. Come to think of it, I'm not even sure the word boyfriend is right. It seems too immature, too insignificant, considering what Colton means to me.

A soft, slightly amused smile lifts Colton's lips. "That's more than okay. In my head I've been thinking that too. I suppose I've just being thinking of you as mine." Pink colors his cheeks, and my heart stutters.

"Caveman style." I bob my head, my grin fast to form. "I like it. I can introduce you like, 'Hey, meet Colton. He's mine.' It sounds possessive as fuck."

A loud, belly-deep laugh shakes Colton's shoulders. "Maybe we keep the 'mine' for when we're in private?"

I can feel it, an honest-to-god pout on my lips. I don't think I've ever pouted in my life, but still, I think we're onto something with the caveman possessiveness.

"How about we table this discussion for tomorrow? A good night's sleep, a gallon of coffee, maybe some Tylenol and you'll be ready to talk about this again."

That sounds mildly reasonable. "Okay. We can do that."

The elevator pings, and we step out into the large foyer. This floor is a shared space with Tony's office, my empty one, and an area for Marybeth, Tony's assistant. There's also a kitchen, shower room, and a large meeting space.

With Death Cab For Cutie still blasting from Tony's office, though, it doesn't feel anywhere near as peaceful as it usually does.

"Quick question." Colton stops me. He searches my gaze as he asks, "Did you talk to Tony about how he's feeling?" Discomfort strains his features, but he powers ahead. "How he feels about you?"

"No," I admit, guilt rattling around in my chest. "He apologized about everything. His treatment of you. Then we knuckled down to business, and…." I shrug, not sure how to admit I'm a coward and am terrified of Tony's possible answer.

"That's okay. If it didn't feel appropriate, then you did the right thing." He glances nervously at Tony's door, from where the music is pouring out. "I just want to know what I'm walking into. Is he going to be pissed off I'm here? Is he an asshole when he's been drinking?"

I part my lips to say no, he's never aggressive or nasty. That he's such a good guy. But I can't say those things, not after yesterday and the spite of his words. The way he tried to hurt me and Colton.

Who am I kidding? There was no try. He did hurt me while making a lasting impression on the man who I care deeply about.

"I want to say no, but…." My shrug says it all.

"Okay. I get it. I'm sure it'll be fine."

Thankful that he's here and he's agreed to be mine, I angle toward Colton and steal a brief kiss. "You're amazing. I'm glad you're here."

Colton's shoulders lose some of their tension as his gaze roams my face. "I wouldn't want to be anywhere else." A mischievous smile curves his lips. "Well, that's a lie. I plan to be eating dinner naked with you in bed in an hour, so let's sort out your friend and make that happen."

We head into the office. The song is coming to an end, so I take the moment to switch it off completely. A glance around the room doesn't reveal Tony dancing. Instead, he's on the sofa, sprawled out and sleeping.

"Well, that's a little anticlimactic."

A snort tears out of me. I shake my head and smirk, looking at Colton. "I'd say you missed out on spectacular dance moves, but…."

He rolls his eyes. "Are you going to wake him? We can't leave him here, right?"

While it wouldn't be the first time either Tony or I have slept in the office, it doesn't feel right to simply walk away after all that's happened. I can't do that to him. "No." Shaking my head, I step closer to Tony. "We need to get him up and in the car. Take him home."

Colton waits near the end of the couch while I bend low, hovering over Tony.

Here goes nothing.

"Tony." I give him a gentle shake. "Come on. Time to wake up and get you home." Another shake. He shifts, his face scrunching. The stink of booze is also seriously strong.

"You got an office chair with wheels around here?"

While Colton's joking, his idea has merit. But I'm sure Tony will just end up falling off.

"Tony, come on. Wakey, wakey. It's time to go."

"Will…." My name's a mumbled slur.

"Yeah, it's Will. I need you to get your ass up so I can take you home."

There's a sliver of white, then the bright blue of his eyes. He blinks them open. "Hey, Willy."

I ignore Colton's chuckle and roll my eyes at Tony. "Can you stand up for me, buddy?"

I think he's trying to nod. I can't quite tell, but it's movement, so I'm going for it.

Taking hold of him, I tug him up, impressed I manage to get him on his feet. Not that he's still. It's like he's standing on a boat in the middle of a storm with the way he's swaying.

"You smell good."

I tense at his words and at how close his face is to my neck. I've never been so viscerally aware of where Colton is, wondering what the hell he's thinking and kind of hoping he didn't understand the slurred words. I flick my gaze in his direction, and judging by how high his eyebrow's arched, it's crystal clear he heard.

"Ha." I laugh it off. "A whole lot better than you, buddy. You stink like a distillery."

"Buddy… baby." He sways so far to the right, my heart spasms, thinking he's going to fall. I hold on tightly, but it's Colton who appears and helps me stand him upright.

"Let's keep focused so you don't fall, okay?" I say.

"I always fall for you."

Holy fucking shit. This right here cannot be happening. Not now. Not ever. And with Tony being smashed…. Shit, once he realizes, he'll be mortified. Then there's the whole thing about Colton being right.

I swallow hard, discomfort rattling around in my chest. "Let's just get you home and in bed."

Even as I say the words, I realize the mistake I made. Tony's gaze is on me. While he's unsteady, his eyes are worryingly focused.

"That's all I've ever wanted, to be in your—"

"And perhaps you need another glass of water," Colton cuts in. He's still holding Tony by his elbow. His dark eyes connect with mine, and I can see he's upset. Not at me. Or at least I don't think so. But let's be honest. This situation is fucked up.

At the sound of Colton's voice, Tony jerks his head toward Colton. It's clear he didn't realize he's here or that he's the reason Tony didn't fall on his ass. "You." A venomous head shake follows. "Shouldn't be here."

Shit. "Tony."

But he's not listening.

"Fuck off back to Lexington."

Colton releases Tony so fast, I struggle to keep him upright. I don't dare let go as I angle to peer at

Colton. The color's disappeared from his face. "I'm so sorry." I shake my head. "He doesn't mean it."

Colton presses his lips together, an all-new level of hurt in his gaze.

"I just need to get him home. Can you grab his phone, wallet, and keys?"

Without a word, Colton walks away.

"They're in the top drawer of his desk," I call out after him. My tone's flat as I try to keep the upset out of my voice. But more than that, I'm fucking furious with Tony. What the fuck is he thinking. Never, not once in twenty years, have I seen this side of him before.

And what the fuck is the Lexington comment about?

Jesus. This weekend has officially become a nightmare. A blemish on the perfect night I spent curled around Colton.

He'll forgive me, right? He's dating me and not my asshole best friend. That has to count for something.

As for Tony…. Anger vibrates my limbs. I'm so fucking furious with myself as well as him. If I'd just called him out this morning, said what I needed to say, none of this would have happened.

Colton's been hurt because of my desire to not make waves.

"I'm going to see if I can get him walking."

Silence greets my words, but at least there's also silence from Tony. If only he'd been mute the whole time.

Frog-marching Tony isn't so bad once we get in a rhythm. By the time we get to the elevator, I've hit the Call button. Less than two seconds later, the doors open. I manage to get him inside and lean him against the wall, my arm still around him.

And then I wait for Colton.

Maybe Tony's things weren't there, so he's having to search. It's not like we can leave without them. I need Tony's keys to get him inside his house. Once upon a time, I had his house key on my ring of keys, but since moving to Collier's Creek, that's no longer the case.

Tony stumbles—over what, I have no idea. His eyes are closed, and his forehead is prickling with sweat.

Fuck. He needs fresh air. If we wait much longer, he's going to hurl.

I hit the button to the parking garage and flick off a text to Colton, letting him know I'll be right back up as soon as I get Tony into the waiting car.

It takes almost ten minutes to get Tony tucked away, in which time my phone vibrates with a text. I finally tug my cell out of my pocket as I head back to the elevator. Exhaustion beats at me. A hangover threatens, and I'm feeling the gross side of sober. For real this time.

All I want is water, Tylenol, and to snuggle in bed with Colton. Beg for his forgiveness and understanding. I'm not sure our naked plans will pan out tonight.

I open my messages as I wave my elevator pass in front of the security pad. The doors open in the parking garage as the message lights up my screen.

> Colton: It's best if I head back to the hotel. Get Tony settled. I'll leave Tony's things at the front desk.

Worry has my stomach clenching. I don't blame him for not wanting to be in the same vehicle as Tony.

This weekend hasn't played out at all like I'd hoped when I invited Colton. While I'm here for business, every other year Tony and I have spent at least three quarters of the time just shooting the shit. It was with that in mind that I thought it was the perfect opportunity to escape with Colton and have some uninterrupted time with him. It was also the chance for him to meet Tony.

Look how well that worked out.

But this is salvageable. It has to be.

It's only Friday night. We still have tonight for me to make him feel good. I'll drown myself in caffeine if necessary. And we still have a whole Saturday, day and night.

Relaxing a little with that knowledge, I turn back toward the town car and shoot off a response to Colton.

> Me: I will see you in 45 mins max.
> Order dinner and I promise I'll make
> this mess of an evening up to you.
> I'm so sorry.

I sigh as I tuck my phone away, wondering how I managed to miss all the signs that Tony has feelings for me. And worse, is so fucking angry that I'm not his.

COLTON

I STARE AT MY PACKED BAG SITTING ON THE LUXURIOUS cotton sheets, count to ten, and grunt.

Fuck.

Am I tempted to get the hell out of here? Grab the last flight of the evening back home? So fucking tempted, my skin itches with the need to run.

But run where? I'm calling Collier's Creek my home, but is it really?

While it checks so many of my boxes and is as close to the picture-perfect life I've always wanted, if Will isn't a part of that, I'm not sure it's where I should be.

I hate that. Hate this feeling of not belonging.

Staring holes through my bag, I pick it up and place it in the large closet. What I want to do is throw the damn thing. But if I broke a coat hanger, I dread to think how much that would cost me to replace.

Rather than storming out, I head for the shower. Calming down is the best place to start. After that, when Will returns, we'll talk this out.

The vision of the papers I found in Tony's desk threatens to unravel my fury, but I can't allow that to happen. Won't. I'm better than this.

That's not to say I'm perfect.

Did I leave the manila folder behind that had my name on it?

I don't even feel guilty that I didn't. Instead, it's burning a hole on the mattress where I threw it after entering the suite.

So much for not giving in to my anger, but that may be better than the hurt clawing at me.

I JOLT AWAKE, SURPRISED I EVEN FELL ASLEEP. THE room is bright, having left the curtains open. As the early morning sun seeps through the windows, the reality hits me right in the solar plexus.

I'm alone. Will hasn't come back to the suite.

Last night I'd been on edge, brushing aside my

frustration and upset. I rationalized every minute he didn't return after his promised forty-five minutes. He'd been drinking, and while he was on the way to sobering up, he could have passed out.

Tony could have been ill, so Will didn't feel it was safe to leave him by himself.

I stare a hole in my phone on the bedside table. It's charging and not on silent. A swipe of my finger on the screen reveals no missed calls, no unread messages.

It's also later than I realized. It's just past seven.

And he's not here.

Still.

Fuck, am I an idiot for still being here? Is it time to tuck my tail between my legs and leave before he returns?

Dealing with the craziness of this weekend seems too big to be unraveling here, in an unknown city. An impersonal hotel suite.

It's going to take comfort and safety, especially when my gaze lands on that damned manila folder.

I'll give him an hour. Ignoring the desire to run to safety is going to be difficult, but Will is worth it. I know he is.

He'll clear up the reason he's not here, why he's not answering his phone, and I'll understand. He'll explain the folio that I never want to see again. The one containing information about my brother, me, the pitchforks running me out of town. A documentation of my parents not being in contact with me since I helped put my brother behind bars.

Nausea curdles my stomach.

One hour. I'll give him that time so we can figure this out.

ONE HOUR TURNED INTO TWO, WHICH TURNED INTO my ass being planted in economy seating on a flight out west. I'd kept my phone on, clinging onto it like a lifeline right to the last minute when I turned on Flight Mode.

That had been closing in on four hours ago.

One connecting flight took me to our local airport, which wasn't at all that local. It left me stuck over an hour away from Collier's Creek. In the end, I'd winced as I agreed to the taxi fee to get my ass home.

I had no one to call. No one to ask to pick me up.

And fuck if how isolated I really am didn't press down on me as each mile brought me closer to town.

The sound of my front door closing with a soft

click reverberates around my brain. I wince at the noise pinging around my aching head.

But I'm home. This small house that I've made my own offers familiarity. And for the first time since yesterday, I take a full, deep breath.

I want to sag against the door, close all the curtains and shut away the world. Get a pint of ice cream and hide in bed. Stinging scratches at my eyes. Straightening my shoulders, I shake my unshed tears away.

I'm better than this. I deserve more than this.

After dumping my bag in my bedroom, I strip and dress in my training gear. While exhaustion thrums through me, I need to work off the heaviness sitting on my chest. I need to sweat and feel the strain of my muscles. Hear the sound of rubber smacking across the ground as I shoot some hoops.

It's the only way I can clear my head. It'll also offer me the distraction I need to work through my unanswered questions and figure out how to react when I come face to face with Will again.

He's a good guy. I know this gut deep, but fuck if I don't feel abandoned. Of course, the irony of me leaving him thousands of miles away isn't lost on me. But I waited longer than my heart and dignity could cope with.

In my defense, I didn't go completely MIA. I left a note, telling him I've headed home and to reach out to me when he returned. That I left the note on top of the manila folder containing all the details of my life…. Well, he could take that however he wished.

It doesn't take long to unlock the school gym and build up a sweat. After thirty minutes using machines and another thirty punishing myself with weights, I've entered the state of calm I seriously need. Thank Christ.

The rubbery scent of the basketball filters through the air, centering me. All I focus on is the rhythmic thumping of the ball against the polished surface. My sneakers squeak through the empty gymnasium, and my mind settles even further.

A satisfying thud as I dribble the ball, preparing to run and take a shot, and I smile. Fuck, it feels good. I focus on the familiar weight of the ball, the leather texture in my grip. The almost melodic dribbling as I charge toward the backboard fills my ears, drowning out the outside world, obscuring my hurt and pain.

With each touch of the ball, my heartbeat steadies. The motion becomes repetitive, almost meditative. I don't care that it's fleeting. For now it's what I need.

Moving in sync with the ball, I smile as the leather leaves my hands and relax at the familiar swish of the net as the ball hits its mark.

Jogging over to get the ball, I slam to a stop when the piercing ring of my phone cuts through my tranquility.

Will.

The uptick of my pulse is a worry. I'm desperate for it to be him so we can figure this out, make this right. I want to wash everything from the past forty-eight hours away. With the exception of our one incredible night together.

Maybe he's already home. Maybe he's desperate to see me. Maybe he's—

Cassius.

Seeing my friend's name is a slap in the face. Not that I don't want to speak to him. Hell, he's my only real friend these days. But still, that it's not Will means that any excuse of my network being down or my phone faulty is no longer a valid one.

"Hey, Cass," I answer, trying to push away the flatness wanting to escape.

"What are you doing right now?"

"Uhm...." I frown and look around the empty gymnasium. "Just finished working out, playing some ball." It's a better explanation than saying what's really going on.

"Google Maps tells me that if you get your ass in your car right now, you can be in Denver in two hours and thirty-five minutes. I think Google is full of shit and doesn't know you have a lead foot, so you can be there in two hours and fifteen."

A laugh startles out of me, and fuck if I'm not grateful Cassius has called me. "And why would I need to get to Denver?"

"Because I'm going to be there in a few hours, asshole."

"You are?" I'm so confused. "Why aren't you in Minneapolis?" His season hasn't started yet, but he doesn't usually travel far from home in the offseason.

"Last-minute charity thing that Ollie wrangled me into," he says, like it's no big deal he's flying around the country to give a little back.

I shake my head, struggling to believe that I've already spent six hours on a couple of flights today. It feels like a million years ago. "Yeah, I'll be there." The words are easy to say. When all the shit went down with my brother, when I'd been questioned by the police to "help them with their investigation," it had been Cassius who'd organized for a lawyer to be at my side within thirty minutes.

While he hadn't been able to sit by my side in the courtroom, his celebrity status too big for that sort of exposure, he'd been my lifeline at the end of my phone.

That he's calling now when it's probably a good thing I'm not by myself seems too serendipitous to ignore.

"Fucking awesome. Bring a suit. I'll text you the details."

And that's Cassius in a nutshell as he whoops, then ends the call.

It looks like I'm heading to Denver.

After grabbing my training gear and showering once I'm home, I collect my suit and my still-packed bag, then head to my car. As I'm throwing my case in the back, Mrs. Hendrix calls out to me.

"You off somewhere?"

"Hey, Mrs. Hendrix. Just a quick trip to Denver to see a friend who's flying in."

Mrs. Hendrix is harmless though in everyone's business. She also happens to be my next-door neighbor. She bobs her head, eyeing my suit bag. "Doing something fancy, it looks like."

My grin is surprisingly quick considering the

deep ache in my heart. But between exercising and Cassius's call, I'm feeling more put together. Sure, I'm still aware of my quiet cell phone, but I don't want to get lost in the hundreds of reasons or excuses for why that is. "Yeah, I'm heading to a charity function. I should get there just in time if I get on the road now."

Rather than taking the hint and saying goodbye, she smiles. "Ooh, somewhere nice? What's the charity for?"

Knowing she'll get wide-eyed, I offer, "At the Ritz-Carlton."

On cue, her eyebrows shoot high. "I hope your suit's dry-cleaned."

I snicker. "It is, thanks, Mrs. Hendrix. I'm not actually sure what the charity event is for, though."

"I made some snickerdoodles this afternoon. Let me get you a plate to take."

Warmth spreads through my chest at her words, her kindness. There's something so special about small-town folk. The knowledge eases something in my gut. Whatever happens between me and Will, this is where I'm meant to be. Surrounded by honest, good people who want me to take freshly baked cookies to the Ritz of all places.

And if things with Will don't work out? The

thought hurts my heart, but maybe, just maybe, there's enough good in the town to keep me here.

"You're too kind, Mrs. Hendrix. But I think the event is catered." The narrowing of her eyes has me saying, "But I'd really appreciate a couple for the drive if that's okay?"

A smile lights up her eyes. "Give me two minutes."

She retreats to her house while I place my suit in my car. I can definitely wait two minutes to accept her kindness.

CHAPTER FOURTEEN

WILL

Knowing you're screwing up while it's happening and feeling powerless to stop it from unraveling further is a position I abhor being in. Allowing it to happen while wishing everything played out differently doesn't mean a thing.

Wishing is for chumps and people with no control.

Apparently I'm both. Neither the sensation nor the moniker sit well.

Excuses and reasons are one thing, but do they really matter when I've let down Colton, the man who's stolen my heart and has left with it to make his own way home? Not only that, but there's Tony as well. There's no getting away from the fact I've let him down too.

Tony's part in it all doesn't matter, nor does both of us wishing he'd done things differently, though since I'm a chump now and everything is spiraling, maybe I'll start burying myself in pointless what-ifs.

The scrunched-up manila folder is in my bag. I should have taken the time to burn it. Instead, I'd grabbed that and my case and jumped in a cab to take me back to Tony's, where I demanded that he explain himself.

I don't give a shit that he pleaded he was looking out for me by running the checks on Colton. Not only did he have no right, but from all that I've discovered, it's impossible to believe he had my best interests at heart.

Tony admitting his love for me, explaining he'd always held out hope that if I ever fell for a man, it would be him, made any sympathy, empathy, or other semblance of emotion beyond anger for the man fall short after this betrayal.

Now, as I edge closer to the outskirts of Collier's Creek, trying to obey the speed limit, guilt has me in her bitter clutches. I left Tony when he begged for me to stay and hear him out.

I shake off the pinch in my chest. As my best friend, the man who's always been there for me, I want to give him a chance, just like I want to shake him and tell him I'm so fucking sad I've never and will never feel that way for him.

But fuck, I'm angry. So damn angry he lied to me. Furious over how he treated Colton. But I'm the asshole who fell asleep after showering the vomit off Tony and maneuvering him into bed. Leaving him had been the plan, but with the state he was in, genuine worry he would throw up and die had held me at his side.

And my phone? I'd searched high and low for the damn thing but without luck of finding it. It wasn't until I returned to Tony's with my bag and the damn manila folder, my heart twisting that Colton had left, that he handed it to me, saying he'd found it water-logged in the shower.

Yeah, that's one way to destroy a phone. A whole lot of water, a cracked screen when it fell from my slacks, because wasn't that a highlight of my night— holding Tony up while I was fully dressed as water poured down on us so he wouldn't drown.

Fun-fucking-tastic.

A new phone was waiting for me when I exited the jet. It stares at me from the passenger seat, still off because I'm too chicken shit to turn it on. I will have to eventually, just so I can make sure Mav is okay. Not that I expect he's been waiting for my call.

When he's with my parents, he's very much at home.

He's also not expecting me home until tomorrow evening.

Colton, though—I need to see him. Need to apologize. Try to make this right.

It's a punch to the gut knowing how badly this weekend spiraled.

His car's not parked outside his house. While my gut clenches, I pull up anyway.

With a deep breath, I exit my car, heading for his front door as I search for signs of life. I'm a hair's breadth from knocking when a "He's not home" has me turning.

It's Mrs. Hendrix. And since she appears to know more than I do, I smile and take a step in her direction. "He's not?"

"He came home a while ago in a taxi, bag in hand."

I somehow hold back my wince, thinking about him traveling from the domestic terminal in Cheyenne in a taxi.

"He's gone again now, though."

I freeze at her words. Legit stop breathing. *Gone?*

One thing I can rely on with Mrs. Hendrix is her

ability to share all her observations and everything she knows.

"He's now driving to Denver of all places, at this time of day if you can believe it?"

"Denver?"

She nods, peacocking a little that she clearly knows something that I don't. "Denver. Heading to the Ritz. I just looked at the place online. Did you know some rooms cost five-thousand dollars a night. A night!" Horror morphs her features. It's probably best I don't let her know I've stayed in a handful of Ritz-Carltons over the years.

But also… why the hell is Colton heading there?

"Did he say why?"

Another smile. "He did. Some sort of charity function. Must be quite a do, since he's taking his good suit."

I have no idea how she knows it's his "good" suit, and it's probably best I don't ask. "Right, well, thanks, Mrs. Hendrix."

As I turn to head back to my car, my brain already ticking over the whys of Colton leaving, Mrs. Hendrix's not-so-subtle cough stops me. Peering back at her, I pause at her arched brow. "Something else, Mrs. Hendrix?"

"Are you going to go after him?"

Momentarily startled, I don't respond.

"I imagine he's going to look mighty dashing in that suit of his."

Of that I have no doubt. "O-kay?" I drag the word out, wondering exactly what she knows, though really, I'm a fool if I think her curtains haven't been twitching over the past couple of months.

"Really, William." A reprimand if ever I heard one. "For the past five years since you've been home, I've seen every emotion cross your face—except one."

Pulse racing, I wait her out, unable to unstick my feet from the ground.

"Carefree joy and love."

The fuck? I swear a mist has rolled into town; that's the only reason my vision has become hazy.

"And I'm not talking about the love you show every day to that precious boy of yours. The way you smile, the way you walk, the set of your shoulders— every part of you shines when I see you with that young science teacher."

Despite the weird mist that's trapped in my eyes, humor whips through me that she's calling Colton young.

"And definitely every time I see you leave this house at all times of the day. I've read enough wonderful romances in my time to know a thing or two about secret liaisons, my boy."

Heat hits my cheeks even as tension eases in my chest. Because she's right. Every single word she's saying is true.

"So, are you really going to let him be swept off his feet, looking all dashing in his good suit, by someone else, or are you going to do something about it?"

The stare she's shooting my way hardens when I don't answer. Honestly, I'm kind of struggling, a little in awe of Mrs. Hendrix and just how amazingly insightful she is. I've only known her as the town's busybody, but hell if I couldn't kiss her right now.

"Well?" she prompts.

"Uhm… yes?"

"Is that a question?"

There's nothing like being schooled by the friendly neighborhood busybody to get you to pull your head out your ass.

"Yes, I'm going to do something about it."

From her nod and smile, it seems I've made the right choice. "Let me just get you a couple of snickerdoodles for the journey, but you need to get a move on. He has an hour's head start."

And so I wait, palm open for my cookies while

I'm already pulling out my new cell, wondering how long it'll take to organize wheels up.

In the end, I settled on rotors rather than wheels. A helicopter was the easiest and fastest way to get to Denver. I only winced slightly when arranging payment. Having not done anything extravagant in so many years, I'm half expecting red flags and phone calls from my bank to make sure my credit card's not been compromised.

Colton is worth it all. The money. The risk of me making a fool of myself. The possibility of him not wanting me there.

After making a call to Marybeth, who doubled as my assistant five years ago, I begged her to find out what was happening at the Ritz and to do whatever it takes to get me in.

Always the miracle worker, she's done just that.

My name is on the charity event guest list. I even now know that Colton must be attending with his friend Cassius, and what's more, the charity is for a transgender support organization. At least my charity donation for the astronomically priced ticket is going to a brilliant cause.

Already in my "good" suit, which I brought to Boston but never had the chance to wear, I take steadying breaths, aware that any second now, the driver is going to be pulling over at the hotel hosting the function.

Jesus, it's hot. How is it so warm? I blow upward, trying to cool down. Sweat is forming in my armpits —never an attractive look (or smell)—and I really need to get ahold of myself.

The only obstacle in my way of making this right is me. If I don't find the right words, I can screw this up. We still need to tell Mav, but he's my and Kelly's boy through and through. He loves me, and he understands heartbreak and loss as well as he understands how lucky it is to fall in love and be loved in return.

It's a lot for a ten-year-old to take on, but he's remarkable. What's more, he adores Colton, not only as a coach, but as someone we've been spending time with.

I deserve happiness, goddammit. I just want to deserve Colton too. Be the man he needs. Be the person who makes him happy.

With that thought, I thank the driver and step out of the car.

A few flashes of cameras fill my vision, but I'm a

nobody in this crowd. It means I can navigate through the entrance quickly, stepping into the luxurious foyer, where I'm directed to the function room for the charity event.

Once there, I give my name, itching to get in. Though what I'm going to do when I get inside and see Colton, I have no clue whatsoever. But in I go, complete with a white card for my table number and a numbered card.

As soon as I enter, I realize I'm beyond fashion-ably late. People are seated around large, opulent tables. The clink of china and the hum of conversa-tion and laughter filters through the low-lit room.

Despite the well-dressed attendees, most screaming of wealth, there's a buzz of energy that surprises me. This event does not look like the frumpy events I've attended in the past. Before I can search, though right now doesn't seem like the time to be dashing around to find Colton, I'm approached by the maître d', who asks to see my card.

As I pass it over with a small smile, I don't stop my gaze from wandering, trying to spot the man who makes my heart race. I follow the maître d' to one of the large round tables. Other than one empty seat, the table is filled, the diners tucking into the food and sipping champagne. Something in my chest eases when there's laughter, genuine smiles, and clearly such an eclectic mix of people.

While I'm not here to enjoy the conversation or the food, knowing I'm not trapped at a table filled with stuffy individuals full of pomp is one heck of a relief. I'm not sure my nerves could cope.

"Sorry for the interruption," I greet, taking a seat while pulling forth what charm I can manage.

"Not at all," a silver-haired woman with bright purple earrings and a wide smile says. "Another friend we've yet to meet. And a handsome one too."

A low chuckle escapes me, and the table joins in. A young guy dressed in a fitted blue suit shakes his head, saying, "You'll have to excuse my mom. She's deep into the bubbles."

"Hush, Alex. The bubbles are deep in *me*. Get it right, kiddo."

"Says my mom to her twenty-five-year-old." Alex's smile is indulgent as he looks at her. Turning his attention to me, he waves a hand around the table. "You missed out on the introductions. So, I'm Alex. I wear this gorgeous badge with pride." He indicates a trans flag on his lapel. "My pronouns are he, him, sometimes they, but tonight, I'm feeling especially he, him."

I bob my head, my smile widening as the table

introduces themselves. It's not a complete distraction from my desperation to locate Colton, but I happily give them my attention.

There really is an eclectic mix around the table of twelve. Alex is here with his boyfriend and his mom, Amber. Carlos, who I learn owns a huge international jewelry franchise—not that he says that his business is huge, but even I recognize the name—is here as an advocate, for the entertainment, and to ogle the array of sporting celebrities who are apparently here.

My thoughts drift to Cassius, who I really should have spent time googling when I first discovered he and Colton were friends. I do know the team he plays for, though, just not what he looks like.

There's also Miley and Tanya, a couple who are a few years older than I am. Mark, who runs a trans youth outreach program, is seriously handsome, but for someone who runs such an incredible program, in this group he appears shy and a little out of his depth. The other four individuals around the table are a group of friends, all in their thirties, and every year they save up to pour their hard-earned cash into a charity fundraiser. One that's "fun and filled with a little mayhem and a lot of hotties," apparently.

Those are Adam's words.

After the introduction, all eyes zero in on me.

I've already downed one glass of champagne but haven't touched any of the food that appeared before me. I figure I need liquid courage to face Colton, despite knowing I should be stone-cold sober.

But in front of this vivacious group, I'm feeling hot under the collar.

"Come on, your turn to spill the goods." Amber leans on her elbows, and while Alex protests with "Mom," it's halfhearted at best.

"I'm here to find the man I'm pretty sure I'm going to spend the rest of my life with."

A collective gasp goes around the table.

"As in you haven't found him yet and you're on the market?" Amber pushes.

I chuckle and shake my head. "I'm definitely off the market. But I screwed up."

"And he's here, your guy?" Adam cranes his neck, looking around the room. Maybe he thinks "my guy" is wearing a neon sign saying *Will's guy* or something.

A huff of air escapes me as I shrug. "I seriously hope so. I was led to believe he's here tonight."

"Is he by himself?"

I shake my head, and there's another collective gasp.

"He's with someone else? Oh my God, I can't handle the drama. We need more champagne." Alex swipes the bottle off the table and pours himself a glass and downs it.

Wide-eyed, I look on, equally entertained and a whole lot bemused by the small group I've become a part of.

"So is he?" Tanya pushes, just as invested as everyone else, it seems.

"He's here with a friend," I clarify. "It's not like that."

"Are you sure?" Amber pipes up, topping up her flute. "I'm sure there was an episode of *Kardashians* like this."

"I'm sure." My lips twitch.

"So what's the plan?" I think it's George, one of Adam's group of friends, who speaks.

I freeze, my lips parting before I snap my mouth closed and shrug. "This was as far as I got."

"You seriously don't have a plan?" Another collective gasp.

Seriously, what's with all the gasping in this place?

"Honestly, it's a miracle I organized a helicopter with thirty minutes' notice to get me here when I did."

Tumbleweed. Apparently, they weren't expecting that disclosure.

"Holy shit. It's like the end of *Pretty Woman!*"

"Uhm—" I attempt, pretty sure this is nothing like that. "He's a science teacher."

But the group's not listening. Instead, they're shouting off the names of movies and TV shows and books with big, dramatic endings. While it's entertaining, it also has me worried.

What exactly is my game plan?

I'm not a big-gesture kind of guy. And this is an apology, a "will you forgive me" moment, not a marriage proposal. And Colton isn't the type of guy for big, public gestures. Or at least I don't think so.

It's time to overshare and put myself in the hands of my new friends.

"I'm thinking more wait until dinner's over and the entertainment—whatever that may be—starts, and then I can seek him out and quietly whisk him away. Ideally to a suite where I can explain and apologize and hopefully kiss him silly before we head home together tomorrow."

"No, no…." Amber claps her hands, but it's the look on her face that makes me nervous. When we all quieten down and she has our full attention, glee fills her expression. "A crude question, but I have to ask, do you have deep pockets?"

"Uhm." I peer around our motley group, at the eleven sets of expectant eyes. "Yes?"

"And you have your paddle?"

My paddle? What the fuck type of charity event—

At my side, Adam lifts the white card, which I now realize is a little paddle-like, that I was handed when I entered.

"Oh, apparently yes, I have a paddle."

"Perfect. If you give me your beau's name, we'll make sure he knows you're here and just how much you want him to be yours."

This is crazy. I still have no idea what the hell she's talking about. The paddle has a number, so I'm assuming there's an auction or something. Shit, what if it's a diamond ring or somet—

"Don't overthink it, Will. Sometimes you have to go all in if you want to win." Amber winks before her gaze turns surprisingly serious. She leans in a little closer, a fierceness on her face. "I want to be super sure, though, that you're serious about your young man. If it was my Alex, I wouldn't want anyone trying to take advantage or end up breaking his heart."

She's in total mom mode. It's a little disconcerting, since she can't be that much older than me.

"Yes, ma'am." I nod quickly and mean every word as I say, "He means everything to me. I want a chance of a future with him."

Adam sniffs beside me, and Tanya blows her nose.

Meanwhile I swallow hard. Fuck it. I've been seated with this group for a reason. It makes absolute sense to follow through.

CHAPTER FIFTEEN

COLTON

For a few split seconds, it's possible to laugh, to get caught up in Cassius and Ollie's banter. That's before there's a punch of sadness to my gut so damn hard it knocks the air from my lungs.

Why does it hurt so damn much?

I haven't given up on Will. A crazy forty-eight hours isn't enough to stop me feeling the way I do for him. Even though I keep telling myself that, it doesn't stop the abrupt hits of pain from coming.

I try to shake it off each time, force my smile to shine brighter, especially when Cassius's concerned gaze lands on mine.

"Have another drink. It'll help."

While I'm not sure that's the best solution here, I

accept the drink Cassius hands me with thanks. The glasses of champagne are going down a little easier.

The last time I sipped champagne was—

"There he is. That dopey, on-your-way-to-be-drunk smile I've missed." Cassius nudges me.

My thoughts of cuddling up with Will cut off abruptly. At least this time I was smiling at the memory. I roll my eyes at Cassius, my smile genuine when I look at him. The guy hasn't changed in all the years I've known him. And I'm hella grateful for that.

"I haven't been that bad."

He arches an eyebrow at me in challenge.

Okay, so my mood is a yo-yo, which is absolutely understandable but not fair at all to Cassius. When he invited me along, it was to catch up and have a good time. What he received instead is a miserable version of myself.

"I'll stop being a sulky slug," I throw back, using a random term that he coined when I first met him at the academy and he was goading Jules Cramdon, who was a miserable bastard.

"Good choice."

"So—" I peer around the table. Most of our group have finished their dessert and are happily indulging in alcohol. Even Ollie, Cassius's team captain, has knocked down several glasses of champagne. I don't think I've seen him drink much in the few times we've met. "—what are these things for?" I wave the card-shaped paddle complete with a number on it.

"For the auction."

I screw my nose up a little at that. This place—my plate—came with a hefty price tag, I'm sure. And absolutely, the event is raising money for a fantastic cause, but not being able to bid stings a little.

From the people sitting at our table, I've discovered there's a real mixed bag of individuals. It's not unnoticeable that the majority have their own wealth to cover the cost of their plate. Maybe if there's a low bid, I can at least attempt to join in. And next payday, perhaps I can just do an online donation.

With the sting of the cab fare I paid earlier, I can't risk digging any deeper into my limited savings.

"Should be a fun one, though." There's a smirk on Cassius's face that I've seen a time or a hundred over the years. One that piques my interest while making me equally anxious.

"The organizers should come by soon to ask for their completed donation from every person in attendance."

I flinch in confusion and scrunch my brow.

"What? What do you mean a donation?" Fucking hell.

Cassius's shrug is annoyingly nonchalant, even as the asshole's lips twitch. "It could be a service—"

"What the hell?" I whisper hiss. "What the fuck auction have you brought me to?"

The fucker bursts out laughing. "You're so fucking easy. Relax, Colton. I mean, if someone was, say, a photographer, they could offer to do a photoshoot. Or if someone was, say, a kick-ass basketball player—"

"Did you call my name?" Ollie's quick on the uptake and leans forward, shooting me a wink.

"Ha ha, asshole. Obviously I'm talking about myself."

My lips twitch as Ollie flips Cassius off.

"As I was saying, a kick-ass basketball player, like myself, could offer a game of one-on-one, or two tickets to our first game."

The pounding of my heart settles a bit at that. No idea why my brain went to blowjobs and putting out, but I never know what to expect from Cassius.

"Okay," I start, "I get it, but don't you think that's something I could have done with knowing about before you invited me?"

A frown dips his eyebrows in confusion. "Nah.

Of course not. Hell, donate your boxers or a lock of your hair. It doesn't have to be serious stuff. Lots of items will be in good fun."

That horrifies me even more. "I'm not offering my boxers."

"Shit, are you not wearing any? I get it. I like to freeball sometimes."

"Cassius." I groan and pick up my glass, draining the contents.

"Sometimes people offer themselves up for a date."

"Are you serious? Like, pimping themselves out?"

"Dude." Cassius's snort captures the attention of those around us. "What is up with you and selling off sexual services?"

Heat flushes my cheeks. I have no idea what's gotten into me, but maybe I should stop drinking. Between my heartbreak, my desperation to cling to hope, the bubbles, and this weird-as-hell weekend, I'm close to the edge.

"I meant a dance, something like that," he clarifies, and I exhale in relief. Okay, that doesn't sound too bad.

Bonnie, a middle-aged woman at my side, leans in, saying, "I'm offering a night out with me in Vegas.

Clint over there has a bag of Doritos stuffed in his jacket pocket."

A huff of amusement falls from me. "Really?"

With a kind smile, Bonnie pats my hand. "Really. Don't overthink it, Colton. Just have fun."

"Yeah, Colton." Cassius bounces his brows. "Just have fun."

I shoot him the stink eye and curve my lips into an imitation of a smile at Bonnie. The woman means well, I'm sure.

Once the tables start to be cleared, the emcee for the evening instructs us to collect a pen and, using the numbered card we were given upon our entry, jot down what we are donating. He explains the proceedings, encourages us to be as wild and whacky, fun or generous as we wish.

We have ten minutes before our donations are collected. Sweat legit breaks out on my brow.

Perhaps I can offer an online tutoring session. Jesus fuck, pathetic much. Not exactly fun, generous, wild, or whacky, is it? It's possible my brain's short-circuiting. I'm not prepared to actually think or be creative tonight. Not after the weekend I've had. Hell, just this morning I was thousands of miles away, nursing a sore heart.

What's Will doing now? Is he home? Has he tried to get in contact? My phone is tucked away in my bag, locked in a room Cassius secured for me. It's probably a good thing I left it upstairs. If not, I have little doubt I would have checked for calls or messages a million times by now.

Shit, five minutes to write something down.

"What are you donating?" I angle to try to get a look at Cassius's paper, but like the child he mentally is, he cups his arm around the card and tells me not to look. "Asshole," I grumble, mildly entertained by his antics.

What to donate?

Maybe I should just say a dance. Not at all creative or exciting, especially since Cassius suggested it, but it means at least the winner can collect their dance today. If not that, the socks I'm wearing, which might possibly have a hole that my big toe keeps getting caught up in, is lowering the bar a little too much.

The cards are starting to be collected. Panicking, I scrawl the words on the card just as someone reaches our table.

All but collapsing back in my seat at just how overwhelmed I feel, I contemplate sneaking off. But a glance at Cassius has me changing my mind. I'm a better friend than this. Tomorrow I'll be back in Collier's Creek, and Will and I can find the time to figure this out.

I have to believe that.

Exhaling, I sit forward, grabbing hold of the champagne and nudging Cassius. "What did you write?" I top up his glass and mine.

"I think it needs to be a surprise."

"Oh God. What did you put? Are you going to do something that's going to have your face plastered all over social media tomorrow?"

Despite his twitching lips, Cassius throws me a deadpan look. "When do I ever get plastered all over—"

At my incredulous expression, he cuts off and huffs out a laugh.

"Okay." He rolls his eyes. "Recently…. When have I *recently* been involved in any salacious gossip?"

Parting my lips to call him out, I pause. Shit. Eyebrows shooting high, I stare at him, roaming his expression. The asshole is right. "Why exactly is that?" I rack my brain, even as he peers at me with a smug smile.

The last thing I recall is the drag show he was

involved in, but that was hardly salacious. It was for his friends' bachelor party. The couple of photographs that leaked were just a group of basketball players in drag, having a good time and celebrating. The images weren't even risqué.

Before that...

Still staring at me, Cassius is apparently waiting for me to get my thinking over. I shake my head. "Seriously, why is that?"

Cassius isn't exactly reckless, but he's been known to make poor choices a time or ten when he's having a good time and trying to keep the party going.

In answer, he shrugs. The smug expression falters a little, and I sit up straighter.

"Are you okay?"

In less than a blink, his smirk is back and he's rolling his eyes. "You love me, I know. But you never need to worry about me." He puckers up, and I don't move fast enough, so he plants a loud, smacking kiss on my forehead.

Lightness settles in my chest at his silliness. "I should be grateful you're not wearing lipstick, I suppose."

A spark dances in his gaze. "I should have thought of that."

"You're ridiculous."

"And you're smiling." His voice dips, taking on a quiet seriousness I rarely hear from him. "I was getting worried there."

Don't you just hate it when people are nice to you? Okay, maybe not hate it, as it's amazing. But when you're already emotionally vulnerable and someone says something kind and considerate… that one thing can be the straw that opens the floodgates.

That is absolutely not how that saying goes, but the meaning remains. This asshole of a friend is awesome, and I'm lucky to have him. I also kind of want to give him a noogie, because if the wind changes, I swear I'm going to cry.

Before I can respond, I'm saved by the emcee. Cassius's gaze is still on me, his gentle concern still easy for me to read. Instead of answering, I squeeze his forearm, sending him my silent thanks.

Apparently, we're getting straight into it.

Numbers are going to be chosen at random, and we're to get our bidding paddles ready. We won't know which lot number is assigned to whom either. That's a relief at least.

And away we go.

By the fourteenth bid, tears are close to rolling

down my cheeks. I'm also close to hyperventilating, not able to quite catch my breath. Lot 6 was a burlesque lesson—online or in the city of the winner's choice—that sold for over three thousand dollars, and Lot 14 is knitted swimwear, with options available. It's the mention of an elephant trunk that has the room rolling. The bid's going strong, and the bidders, as well as those looking on, are having fun with the jokes and banter.

I really needed this.

When the bidding wraps up, we move onto a freshly made Boston cream pie, delivered right to your door. My laughter slides away, and my heart pangs. The bid's at two hundred dollars, and I can't help it. I lift my hand and raise my paddle.

I know I have Cassius's attention, but I can't look at him. The bid goes up and up, and we're close to the seven-bid limit: the organizers' way to ensure fast bids and that we don't fall asleep from boredom from so many lots. I swallow hard, placing my paddle down. But it's great. More money for the amazing charity. If it's possible to think through gritted teeth, it's totally what I'm doing.

"Two thousand dollars." Cassius lifts up his paddle as he shouts out the figure.

"And sold to 187."

I turn to him. He gives me a side-eye and one of his sweet, carefree shrugs and leans in close, saying, "It better be the best pie you ever have."

I don't have the heart to tell him it's cake.

As we're drawing to what must be the end, it's super clear why they implemented the number of max bids. The way the servers are constantly refreshing bottles and topping up drinks makes sense too.

They've yet to offer my lot up, but I'm well on my way to being merry, so by the time the emcee says, "And tonight's final lot...," a wide smile is splitting my face.

Obviously we're not meant to say who donated what at this point, but everyone on our table shared either before or as soon as their lot was announced.

My table cheers as soon as the emcee speaks. Yeah, we're definitely all super tanked up on champagne.

The emcee glances our way, shaking his head with an amused smile. "Lot 190, a lap dance."

My body locks up. *What?*

I'm mildly aware of Cassius at my side, snorting a laugh so violent, I think he might collapse.

I part my lips, wide-eyed and so fucking confused. Last dance. I wrote *last dance*.

But with the opening bid being two thousand dollars, I can't do anything but sit here in horror and hope that the ground swallows me whole.

WHAT THE EVER-LOVING FUCK?

Lap dance. It takes my brain far too long to catch up. It takes Amber prodding me, the whole of our table staring at me, to snap me out of it.

"What bid number are they on?" My question's frantic.

"Five," Adam answers.

Fuck. I have to time this right. Seven bids. I can't be six. No fucking way. But seriously, *lap dance?* What the hell is Colton thinking?

The emcee's "Fourteen thousand dollars," has me shooting my paddle up so damn high and shouting, "Fifty thousand dollars," even as I hear two more bids. Fuck. What were they? I should have said a hundred.

Tension vibrates my limbs as I stare at the emcee. He touches his ear, and I can only assume he has an earpiece in. "Please hold, everyone. We're just capturing the bids and working out who the successful bidder is."

The whole room comes alight with laughter and conversation. Except for our table. It feels like we're in this together as we collectively hold our breaths.

The emcee nods at whatever he hears. "Thank you for your patience." The room settles. "It seems we have a tie. Two bidders with the same bid offer."

My hand shoots up. "One hundred thousand." Jesus, I'm going to get escorted off the premises with my desperation.

If the emcee is surprised, he doesn't show it. Instead, a wide smile, friendly and conspiring, appears on his mouth. "Well, that's one way to solve it, but we need an agreement from the collective or maybe from the individual who donated the final lot. Shall we see what they think first?"

The room applauds and cheers, a few hollering, "Yes." Holy hell. Colton is going to kick my ass for all the attention directed his way, but hello, lap dance. I can't get my head around why he would do that.

There's movement to the far right of the room.

My heart skips a beat. I can't see what's going on, but I can only assume it's Colton.

Confusion slams into me when a man bounds to the stage. It's definitely not Colton.

The guy's tall, broad-shouldered, wearing a tailored suit. His skin is dark and gleaming under the bright lights of the stage.

"That's Cassius Britton," Adam gasps, his voice breathy. I can barely hear him under the rowdy applause and cheers.

"What?" I zero in on Colton's friend, wondering if Amber got her intel wrong. My gaze snaps to hers, and she looks just as confused as I am.

Fuck. Did I bid on a lap dance from Cassius? Mortification slams into me, though there's a bubble of laughter hovering in my chest at the whole ridiculousness of the situation.

"Thank you for the generous bids." Confidence pours through Cassius's words. "Perhaps the show should be for you all tonight, especially after a record bid. What do you say?"

What on earth is happening?

At the loud hollers, Cassius forms a smug smile. "In that case, let's invite the bidder up to the stage. What do you say?"

Amused, I gasp out a surprised laugh. In any

other situation, I'd be sticking my ass like glue to this chair and telling the organizers they can have the money as a straight-up donation.

But color me curious. Amber was certain about the bid number. She doesn't seem like the type of woman to settle with misinformation.

Intrigued, and with my group cheering me on, I stand, button my jacket, and make my way to the stage.

A chair has been organized by the time I get there. I almost stumble, my stomach lurching. He's not going to really give me a lap dance, right?

When Cassius spots me at the side of the stage, he smirks, strolls ridiculously leisurely on his long legs in my direction, and invites me up. On unsteady feet, I do so, the lights blinding.

He can't know who I am, surely. It's possible that Colton's shown him a photograph, but if that's the case, he'd be sending animosity my way, right?

With the lights on me, I forcibly relax my shoulders, trying my hardest not to look like I'm about to bolt.

"Welcome." There's a heavy hint of flirtation in Cassius's voice.

"Thanks." I latch on to my days of dealing with clients, ensuring carefree amusement tinges my words as I say, "I'd say it's great to be here, but looking at the chair center stage, I'm not so sure."

Laughter fills the room.

"Now, don't be afraid of the chair. It won't bite you."

Another round of laughter.

"But I do need to share a little secret with you all." Cassius peers around the room. "Your winning lot wasn't donated by me."

The audience stirs.

"I know, I know, you'd all love to see me in action." Cassius is a complete showman. I can only imagine how he handles the crowd at a game. "But… it is one of my closest friends, and I wouldn't be being a good guy if I didn't check out who it was so eager to win his lovely… lot."

So much for anonymity, I think dryly.

"Saying that, maybe his shyness will work in my favor. I've been known to be an excellent team player."

While the audience laughs, I startle and flick wide eyes at him. Fuck.

"Uhm… nope. No."

I snap my attention toward the bright lights. I can't see shit, but that voice.

"No, I've got this, thanks, Cass" is hollered out.

Out the corner of my eye, I see genuine surprise flash in Cassius's expression. He schools his reaction quickly.

"And there we have it, party revelers. My friend has accepted the challenge, which means I'm going to hand you back to the very capable emcee and let him wrap up the proceedings."

He bows somewhat elaborately and indicates for me to lead the way off the sidesteps. Once we're offstage, the emcee starts talking and explaining about payment and collecting winning bids.

There's a heavy throb sounding in my ears as I follow him. My focus is on the direction I'm being led as I search for Colton, desperate to lay my gaze on him.

"Before we get to my friend…." He pulls me to a stop.

I hold back my sigh, wanting to hurry up and get to Colton. What I don't want to do is piss Cassius off, though. "Yes?"

"The bid you offered…. I'm happy to take on the bid so the charity doesn't lose out."

The fuck? He wants a lap dance from his friend?

"His lot wasn—"

"Cass." He's interrupted, and it's by the best voice I've heard all day.

Cassius turns, revealing Colton. There's no holding back the catch of my breath.

"It's fine. I can honor the lot."

"You can?" Confusion has him wide-eyed.

"Yep. I'm assuming this gentleman just needs to pay." An arched brow and a flash of humor is sent my way, and fuck if my pulse doesn't take off even as my heart melts.

"Yeah, sure." I tug out my phone, and Colton's gaze slams to it. "I'll need to set it up properly." I lift it up, saying pointedly, "New phone. It was delivered to me when I got home."

A spark of emotion appears in the depths of his deep-brown eyes. "Okay." His words are quiet. "That explains a few things."

"What does?" Cassius glances between the two of us.

Ignoring him, I step forward, closer to Colton. "I'm so fucking sorry for letting you down." I want to reach for him, hold him tight, whisper all the words in his ear. The difficulty of holding back is a visceral force, but I need to explain what happened first.

He needs the truth of it all.

"Please let me explain. Let me find a way to earn your trust again."

"Holy shit. You're Will, right?" Cassius's question

draws my attention. His friendly smile is long gone. He directs a hard stare instead my way before he glances at Colton. "Thank fuck. I really thought you were going to give a stranger a lap dance. About gave me a heart attack."

Despite the heaviness, Colton's lips twitch. "I couldn't miss the opportunity to tease you a little."

"Asshole. Well-played. You good for me to leave you to it?" His wary gaze flicks my way as he sizes me up.

I offer a closed-lipped smile, wondering if we will ever get to the stage where we can joke about him flirting with me.

God, I hope so.

"Yeah, thanks, Cass." Colton's eyes shift to his friend. "Seriously, thank you."

He bobs his head before glancing at me. He's studying me intently. "Was the pie to do with you?"

I huff out a quiet laugh. "Yeah." My gaze connects with Colton's. "Who won it?"

"That'll be me." Cassius whips his head back to Colton. "I'll be keeping the damn pie since all this is going on."

"Have at it. I know how much you love *pie*." A secret smirk passes between us.

"Rightly so. Okay, I'm going to drink and dance. Meet for breakfast before you leave tomorrow?"

"Definitely." Colton squeezes his arm lightly, and Cassius leaves us to it.

"Can we go somewhere to talk?"

"I have a room."

Nerves dance in my stomach as we find the maître d' so I can organize payment. I keep my hands shoved deep in my pockets the whole time, anxious for the time I can touch him again.

I DON'T HOLD ANYTHING BACK.

If I was telling the story of this whole clusterfuck of a weekend with anyone else, about how events snowballed, I'm sure they wouldn't believe me. With Colton being witness to most of it, I see what I think is understanding. At some parts that I recollect, he bobs his head, and at times, he raises his brows. At others, the parts that make me wince, his frown is severe.

"That I didn't see it…." I shake my head, not sure I can express just how angry I am at myself for not seeing how Tony felt. Huffing out a breath, I don't pull my gaze away from Colton.

He's sitting on the armchair next to the hotel window in the room Cassius arranged for him. Exhaustion radiates from him. It's darkened the area under his eyes. It doesn't make him look any less handsome.

"I didn't read it." It's the gargantuan tutu-wearing elephant in the room. "That he did that—" A surge of anger has me cutting myself off. This isn't a time for such emotions. I want to let all that go, simply bask in how Colton makes me feel. Enjoy the way his smile lights up his face when I've done something that makes him happy.

Life's too short for anything else.

I exhale and try again, ensuring I capture Colton's gaze and don't lose it. "I didn't know what it was. I looked at the first page…." It's hard to keep going, but my cowardice helped get me in this situation in the first place. "When I realized what it was… a dive into your past, your history, I stopped immediately."

The pounding of my pulse almost echoes in the otherwise silent room.

"I would never betray your trust like that." Urgency, honesty, absolute conviction rings through my words. "The photograph fell out."

It was seeing the image of Colton's bruised face

that set a fire in me and had me racing to Tony's. It was only the haunted look in Colton's eyes staring back at me from the photograph that prevented me from doing something I would have been ashamed of.

I could have ended up being like the type of person who did that damage to Colton in the first place. How could I live with myself if I'd folded under my fury? Look either Mav or Colton in the eye again?

Short bursts of breath make my chest heave.

Colton remains still, the shadows in his eyes still there. His fingers twitch, and his gaze moves. It tracks the tear trailing slowly down my cheek.

"Is there a way for me to fix this?" I have to know, and if there is, I'll move mountains to make it happen.

"You're a good man." His words have me holding my breath. "Despite everything, I knew you were trying to do the right thing. In your shoes…." He pauses before lifting a shoulder in a small shrug. "If that was me and Cass, I know I would have done the same thing. Got him home. Made sure he was okay. I know I would have. I probably would have been tempted to throw basketballs at his head to try to knock some sense into him maybe." The twitch of his lips is halfhearted at best, but it's something.

"You are so important to me. Thursday night meant everything." Jesus, was that just two nights ago?

How on earth did we end up here?

Which is completely and absolutely rhetorical. Answering that question will just fire me up again.

"I hate that I hurt you. Hurt us," I continue. "It's something I promise to try to never do again."

There's a tiny glimmer of a smile at my words. "Thank you for not promising that you'll never hurt me again."

I bob my head, understanding his meaning. Shit happens. Feelings get hurt. Stupid decisions can be made. To promise that those things will never happen would make me a liar.

"I hate that you were hurt this weekend too." Sincerity holds his words steady.

A tremble starts in my hands with the longing to reach out to him. I clench my fists, respecting that he needs the physical distance between us.

"What's going to happen between you and Tony? Your company?"

Expelling a heavy breath, I shake my head, sagging

a little on the small couch I'm perched on. "This morning I was close to making calls to sell my shares and cut Tony out of my life." The words hurt to say. "Now, I just don't know. I can't rush into any decisions. Tony was wrong on so many levels. Unforgiveable on even more. I don't know how to navigate that." I swallow hard before saying, "I wouldn't have survived Kelly's short illness or her death without his support."

Colton presses his lips together.

"What?" I prompt, not wanting him to hold anything back.

There's a slight hesitation before he says, "I think you need to give yourself more credit. I can't imagine what losing Kelly was like for you, and I don't doubt Tony supported you, but whether you realize it or not, Will, you're a remarkable guy."

The stumbling of my heart has me sitting up a little straighter.

"There is nothing you wouldn't do to make sure Maverick is happy, and since your love makes him happy, even if you didn't have anyone to give you a helping hand, you would have got through it. Not only because you're incredible, but because you love that boy of yours." Shining eyes peer back at me. "I hope you'll tell me so many stories of Kelly so I can feel like I know her, but even now, I can confidently say, she'd be so proud of you."

Fucking hell.

How can I hold back after that?

I'm on my feet, then on my knees before him. Emotion stills my words, but that's okay. He scoots off the chair and lands on his knees before me, winding his strong arms around me.

I wrap everything I feel into my hold, pulling him impossibly close and inhaling deeply as I dip my face to his neck. "Thank you" doesn't sound significant enough, but it's all that I have. That and... "I love you, Colton. So fucking much."

At my words, he squeezes me but won't let me pull away. I let him have this moment. He can have as many as he wants if he eventually says he'll still be mine.

"The photo...." The words are whispered, reaching me with ease since we're wrapped around each other. My heart stutters as I wait for the rest of his words.

When he loosens his grip and pulls away, I grasp onto his hands, not wanting the distance.

Our gazes meet, and while pain still lurks in his, there's also determination burning brightly. Without a doubt, I know he's strong enough to find his way through any looming darkness.

"That was the result of me trying to stop my brother from stealing the proceeds of a work basketball fundraiser."

Shock reverberates through me, and I grip his hand tighter, letting him know I'm here for everything he wants to share.

"After he put me in the hospital with the damage you saw on my face, a cracked rib, and a concussion, he made off with almost ten-thousand dollars in fundraising money. When he was caught, he didn't have any drugs on him, but I told the police where they were stashed and later attended his trial. He's served four of his eight-year prison sentence with no chance of early parole."

Words buzz around my brain while emotion floods my system. "Jesus." It's all I can manage. "I'm so sorry you went through that." And fuck if it doesn't make the whole drama surrounding us this weekend seem completely bullshit and insignificant. "You are incredible."

A startled laugh with a chased "What?" tumbles out of him.

"You are. Just look at you. Look at how…" I grasp around for the right word. "… resilient and just amazing you are. You went through all that and still get up each day, teach kids, some of whom I'm sure don't appreciate you."

Pink touches his cheeks, and more lightness settles in his gaze. "I do teach some assholes."

"Exactly. And yet you do it anyway, and you coach our uncoordinated team."

His chuckle wraps around us, lighting him up from the inside. "I've got a couple of star players."

"You do all that for free, in your own time, out of the goodness of your heart."

He snorts. "And a lot of pressure from the principal."

I roll my eyes at him. "And through it all, you're self-deprecating rather than basking in the praise of truly understanding just how fucking remarkable you are."

He peers back at me with tenderness, and I think he's finally starting to get it.

"If I wasn't already in love with you, what I just discovered would have made me fall."

Colton swallows hard, his eyes misting. But there's a playfulness dancing in their depths that I love. "Fall how?"

I smirk and lean in. "Completely." I brush my lips against his. "Utterly." I ghost the word over his mouth before dotting another kiss there. "Irrevocably." I capture him in a kiss, drinking him in, savoring his warmth, his stuttering breath, beyond grateful that he's opened himself up to accepting my apology for all that's passed between us.

He pulls away, gasping. Frustrated, I groan, chasing his mouth.

Stopping me with his palm on my cheek, his gaze roams my face. "Anyone willing to pay a hundred grand for a lap dance must be all of those things."

Which reminds me.

"Did you know I was there? Is that why you chose a lap dance?" Call it wishful thinking, as that's exactly what it is.

His loud laugh and shake of his head nips that theory in the bud immediately. "I didn't know you were there." At my narrowed gaze, he smirks, stroking his thumb over my cheek. "What is a worry is that my handwriting is so bad *last* was read as *lap*. It was the *last* dance of the night."

"Holy shit." A chuckle tumbles out of me. "Seriously?"

"Seriously."

I shake my head. "I'm just grateful I found out about the event."

"Mrs. Hendrix?"

"Of course."

"We owe her a bunch of flowers."

I absolutely agree. But right now, I really want Colton naked and to be under him.

With the way his gaze heats, it seems he has the same idea.

I reach for him, fingers landing on the hem of his shirt. When he moves his hands to mine to stop me, I pause immediately.

"I love you, Will."

Wings take flight in my chest, fluttering around so fast that I think without Colton's hands on me, I could float away.

"Perhaps the lap dance can be round two." There's a definite tease in his voice. "For right now, I just want to hold you close and show you all the ways you really are mine."

CHAPTER SEVENTEEN

COLTON

I don't release Will's hand the entire journey, never more grateful that I drive an automatic.

The journey home is filled with quiet conversation and gentle touches. I'm aware of every move and every breath, and even after last night and the intensity of our lovemaking and blowing my load down his swallowing throat this morning, I can't stop touching him.

Since we left after our breakfast with Cassius and Ollie, it's only just past midday when we pull into Will's street.

"How have I not been to this part of town before?" Trees line the sidewalk, and long drives lead to large, mostly older homes, all with a Colonial feel to them. It's a nice street with a large half-acre block.

"I imagine it's got something to do with you hitting the ground running when you moved into Collier's Creek." The stroke of his thumb across my wrist follows his words, and fresh goose bumps break out.

How is it that such a simple touch is filled with so much promise?

"This is me." He indicates a home that's cookie-cutter perfect. Not only does it have a legit white picket fence, but there's an impressive wraparound porch, white-washed shutters framing the windows, and a neatly maintained lawn. The basketball hoop above one of the two garage doors makes me smile.

While the other homes on the street are nice, Will's place is next level. And I finally get to see it.

"You weren't exaggerating about the renos." At least now I understand how he afforded it. He could have built a mansion or something ostentatious, but that he didn't, that he brought a beautiful home to life, is very much in line with what I know about Will.

What I love about him.

Even thinking the words as I pull up into his drive has my heart flipping over.

It's the first time I've ever uttered those words to another man. Since I did so last night, the words keep wanting to spill out, almost begging me to say them again and again.

But that's what this man does to me.

He makes me feel wanted and needed and so damn happy. I want to shower him in love and affection.

"I have tons of before photos. I'll show you them sometime. But for now, how about I give you the tour?"

"Sounds good." Another stuttering of my heart follows.

Unbuckling, he leans over, drawing my gaze back to him and away from the house. "I love you," he says, his gaze roaming my face. The tender uplift of his lips along with his sweet words will always be my undoing.

Capturing his lips, I glide my mouth over his. I sink into the connection, sigh into his touch when he cradles my cheek, groan when his tongue—

"Dad?"

We jolt, shifting apart so fast, the momentum is off. My elbow smacks into the steering wheel with a crack that hits the horn. I wince at the noise and the sting of pain in my elbow. From Will's grunt, he either hit his head or maybe pulled a muscle with the speed he moved.

"Shit, are you okay?"

Wide-eyed, he's rubbing at his neck, but his gaze isn't on me.

I have to look. Follow his gaze even though I'm pretty sure I know what I'm going to see. The plan was for Will to sit down with Maverick tonight and tell him that we're dating. Tomorrow, we were going to have dinner together and make sure Maverick is okay with this new development.

Fuck.

Peering back at us through the front window is a furrow-browed Maverick, a smirking gray-haired man in his late sixties, maybe early seventies, and a tender-eyed woman who, it's clear even from this distance, shares the same smile as her son.

Will's quiet "Are you okay to meet all the family as my boyfriend?" catches my attention completely.

Not seeing any panic staring back at me loosens something in my chest. "Yeah, if you're sure."

"I'm 100 percent sure of you." He reaches for my hand, having lost it in our frantic separation. A light squeeze settles my nerves a little more. "I might need to talk to Maverick by myself."

"Yeah, of course. Whatever you need." I'm viscerally aware of our audience, but at least Maverick hasn't raced away.

"Thank you." And then he's exiting the car and I'm scrambling to follow him, not sure what expression to land on. I think I end on an awkward "yes, you caught me making out, but can you blame me?" smile just as Will says, "Hey, now this is an unexpected greeting."

"We can see that, son." Since his dad's still smirking, I edge around the car, slowing my long gait a little.

"Maverick needed his basketball pump." His mom's voice is calm as she peers at her son before flashing her attention to me.

Since there's nowhere for me to go but to stand in front of my car, I do so, that same weird smile on my face. Jesus, I hope I don't look constipated. With a brief nod to Will's mom, I focus on Maverick.

He's the person who matters.

Rather than staring at his dad, his assessing gaze is on me.

"Have you put in so many hours of basketball that it needs pumping up again already?" It's all I can manage to say while not knowing what he saw or how he must be feeling.

Though, trying to fool myself into thinking he might not have seen me with my tongue down his dad's throat is pointless. There was no chance anyone passing by couldn't see, and since the three members of Will's family were smackdab in front of the car staring at us….

The seconds of quiet seem to stretch. It feels like a lifetime of awkward beats before there's even movement. Maverick turns his attention to his dad. With his brow no longer scrunched in confusion, I think we're all waiting for this one child's reaction. Undoubtedly, he can change everything.

"Are you and Coach boyfriends?"

I lean against the hood of my car, not sure what to do with my hands. Will's standing next to his son, side-on so I can see his face. When his gaze connects with mine and a tender, reassuring smile forms, I release a shaky breath as I tilt up my lips in solidarity.

"Yeah. I asked him this weekend and somehow managed to talk him into saying yes."

I clamp down on my snort, my mind snagging on all the conversations we've shared this weekend and everything that's gone down. I wait for the hurt of all that's happened to bubble up, but it doesn't.

There's no need to hold on to it, especially not when the only people who matter in our relationship are the two of us and Maverick.

"It's probably a good idea you took the jet, then.

He might have said no otherwise." There's no venom or sass in his tone. Not even obvious humor.

Surprise and amusement ripple through me. A huff of a laugh spills from Will. His parents chuckle.

But Maverick hasn't finished. "How else could you get someone so *cool* to be your boyfriend." And when he bounces his brows, I know it's going to be okay.

"Hey!" Will snags hold of his son around the waist, and Maverick folds into laughter. It's loud and gasping, the teasing behind his words finally hitting their mark.

A shaky breath later, I flex my fingers, absorbing the relief and the break in tension that coiled around me.

As Will stays locked in a tickle fest with Maverick, his parents step a little closer.

His mom is the first to reach out to me. Startled by her tight hug, it takes me a second to reciprocate. "It's so wonderful to meet you." She presses a light kiss to my cheek before pulling away. "I'm Bess and this is Clay. We're responsible for the two numbskulls who you're bravely taking on." Her smile is gentle; her words are pointed.

"Not brave. Just lucky," I respond.

From the softness in her expression, it's the right

thing to say.

"Colton." I introduce myself and reach for Clay's hand. "Good to meet you, sir."

His grip is strong, friendly. "You too. And Clay is more than okay. Did you have a good trip?"

How to answer that?

"You're back much earlier than we expected," he adds.

Will saves me from responding by saying, "It was eventful." At the curiosity in his parents' eyes, he moves to stand next to me, his arm going around my waist in a move so natural, it's like we've done this a million times. "Another time."

His parents nod, apparently satisfied with his response.

"Since you're all here, do you want to put the grill on, Dad, and the both of you stay for a while?" The hand on my waist squeezes, and I sigh into the touch.

"Lunch sounds great," I add, making it clear that while this is all unexpected, I'm more than happy to go with the flow.

"In that case, that sounds great." Bess nods and turns to her grandson. He has the garage door open and is riffling around the shelves. "Maverick, let your pops get that before you drag a box on your head." She spins on her heel, Clay following close behind.

Is their acceptance really that easy? How is this all falling into place?

"You okay?"

With us both leaning on the hood of my car, I don't have to tilt quite as far to make eye contact with Will. "Yeah, I think so." Seeing concern flicker to life, I quickly amend, "I am. I suppose I'm just waiting for the other shoe to drop."

"Maverick's a good kid."

"I know that. He's like his dad that way."

The tender smile he shoots me makes my knees weak. The power this man has over me, how he can make me feel, should come with a warning label. Or maybe a signal. It would make me better prepared for his sweet affection.

"When Kelly passed, she left us so many notes and letters."

"Oh wow. Really?"

"Yeah." A light shake of his head precedes him saying, "She was so damn organized and always preparing for the future, especially knowing she wouldn't be around. She left Maverick one for every year of his birthday. When he turns twenty-one, it'll be his last." A fond sadness rolls off him.

"She really was an incredible woman." And to achieve all that in the six weeks she had before passing. Warmth for the woman I'm so grateful for spreads through my chest.

"She was. She also—and I suppose I did, too, since Kelly insisted—prepared Mav for this day."

The pounding in my ears picks up speed. Questions burn in my brain.

"She prepared him for you."

My breath catches.

"Mav's always known that one day I could meet someone—a man or a woman—who I'd share my heart with. In her letters, Kelly celebrated the time that would happen, encouraged Mav to share my joy when it did."

"Fucking hell, Will." Dampness coats my cheeks. This right here is when that warning system should come into effect.

"Hey." His chuckle is light and affectionate. Moving to stand before me, he smiles. Positioned like this, we're at the same height. It means it's easy for him to lean in and capture my mouth.

I taste my tears, knowing he can too. It doesn't hold either of us back as we embrace, our mouths sliding tenderly together. When the kiss ends naturally and we continue to embrace, his face snug where he seems to like being the most—inhaling the skin at my neck—I close my eyes, savoring the man in my arms.

Gratitude for Kelly and the remarkable gift she left me thrums through my veins.

"I'm going to head to the store, maybe take Mav with me," Will says as he leans away.

"Absolutely. Will he tell you if he's not really okay?"

"Definitely. And you have nothing to worry about. Mav thinks you're great."

"Cool was the word he used."

He chuckles. "That's because he's an asshole and mocking me. But he still thinks you're great."

Knowing that eases some of the tightness around my chest.

"You going to be okay alone with my parents?"

It's easy to say yes. There was no deception in his parents' easy acceptance—of that, I am sure.

"Perfect." He steps fully away and reaches for my hand. "I still want to give you a tour of the house first."

I go willingly, sliding my hand into his, certainty accompanying every step I take, hand in hand with the man I intend to spend the rest of my life loving.

I DON'T WANT TO LOOK. TEMPTED TO COVER MY FACE and peer between my fingers, I instead curl my hands up next to my thighs.

The game is fast. Intense. Each pass, each shot the Bisons take, and each point against them raises my anxiety another notch.

The freshmen team is on fire, and with the way practically the whole town is cheering for the young players, you'd think this was a senior sport, maybe even a college game. It's so not that, but for almost five years, the Bisons have been playing together with Colton as their coach, and this game right here is their first official high school game.

I wince when a player from the Wildcats collides with Tennyson. Our forward is nothing if not tenacious. He jumps right back up and races into position, open for a pass.

These kids have come such a long way, largely thanks to Colton never giving up.

A pensive expression has his brow scrunching as he stands on the sidelines. He's never been one to shout or holler. Not that he's not passionate. Just the thought of how passionate my husband is sends my heart speeding and shoots a flash of heat over my skin.

How much longer is left before I can celebrate properly?

A glance at the clock shows just a minute left. Between the rest of play, the cleanup, the promised pizza that Mae and Fiona are organizing for the boys at their restaurant, maybe I can be riding him in a couple of hours, if I'm lucky.

"Yes!" I'm out of my seat and cheering loudly as Mav sinks the ball through the net. I clap, my hands heating with the intensity of the motion. At my side, Dad grips me on the shoulder.

"Will you just look at that kid." Pride colors his words, and I feel them deeply.

"I told Sheriff Morgan to expect a lot of noise in town after tonight's game," Mom says, her focus never drifting from the action on the court.

She's not going to be wrong. It's taken a while for the town to warm up to basketball. In fairness, when the kids were younger, their games weren't the most riveting, but now, they're incredible. They train so hard and are dedicated, barely even having an offseason.

Colton and I have embraced Mav's enthusiasm and his skill, and even though it's clear to all of us there're no expectations for Mav to grow another foot over the next few years, he's still determined to play college ball. Montview Academy has always been his goal since the moment Colton told him about the summer training camp.

The clock's ticking down.

Tucker intercepts the ball, and we're on our feet. We've already got the game in the bag since we're fourteen points up, but still…. Tucker pushes forward with control, certainty. Just when I think he's going to shoot, he passes to Mav. The pass lands true, the leather finding its mark before my son dribbles, dodges, and lets the ball fly.

The sway of the net as the ball passes through signals an uproar of hollers around the small gymnasium. A second later, the buzzer goes.

Grinning, I clap loudly before hugging my parents. Hearty claps land on my shoulders and back, congratulating me on both Colton and Mav's win.

"You go down. We'll wait here until the crowd settles." Dad indicates that I should leave. I hover a moment. All that does is earn me a disgruntled eyeroll. "I said I'd sit and wait."

Aging is hard as hell, and even though there's nothing in particular to be concerned about with Dad's health at the moment, seventy-six is creeping up fast, and I still worry.

"Okay." I shoot Mom a pointed look, knowing she'll keep him in line. It'll be all too easy to be jostled in this crowd.

As soon as my feet hit the court, I seek out Mav. He's just finishing fist-bumping the Wildcats, bobbing his head and controlling his grin. At the last "Good game," he spins, grabbing hold of Tucker, and the two hug it out, no longer holding back their glee.

Leaving him to celebrate with his friends, I cast my gaze around the busy court, searching for Colton. My husband's grinning, talking to his assistant coach, Jordan. Was I upset I was usurped out of my role two years back? Honestly, no.

Colton and Mav sharing something they're both passionate about without me interfering has been the best thing ever. Sure, Colton is very much Mav's coach at practice and at games, but their bond and love is so incredible.

Taking my time to get to Colton, courtesy of speaking to and congratulating the other parents, I never drop my smile. Flashes of red jerseys dance in my peripheral, the FortressCyber logo proudly sponsoring the team printed on their chests.

Tony and I are currently finalizing the sponsorship of a larger gymnasium, one with a lot more seating available to our community, with Collier's Creek's principal. We're almost ready to submit the agreement, and hopefully in eighteen months, the extension will be made, and come Mav's senior year, I expect the volume from maximum capacity will raise the roof.

I pull out my phone with thoughts of Tony. It took two years for us to finally find our way back to each other. And now, considering all that's passed and the lives we're leading, I'm grateful we got there. A photo of the scoreboard accompanies my message.

> Me: I suppose a honeymoon is the only possible excuse for missing your godson's high school debut. He was incredible.

I don't expect a response. I have no idea what

time it is in New Zealand, but since he's only on day three of his honeymoon, the last thing he should be doing is checking his cell. And knowing Brock, he will have hidden away all electronic devices as soon as they boarded the plane.

"Hey." I team my greeting with a gentle squeeze to Colton's waist.

He spins to face me, then wraps me in a hug, pulling a chuckle out of me. I hug him tightly before easing back, but not releasing him fully until I steal a brief kiss.

"Congratulations. I'm so proud of you."

Emotions have him tightly in their grasp. Knowing he needs a minute, I reach out to Jordan at his side and shake his hand. "Congrats. The boys did you proud."

Jordan grips my palm, jubilation on his features. "That they did. And Mav..." His smile seems to stretch. "...that kid of yours is something special."

I beam. "He really is. A mix of talent and a dad who practices all hours of the day with him"—I squeeze Colton lightly—"though I wish I could take a little credit."

Jordan is called away by his brother Coop. I tell him we'll catch up at the restaurant and focus once again on Colton. He's more together now.

"You okay?"

He shakes his head, clearly at himself, and rolls his eyes. "Yeah. Just got me. Took me by surprise."

I bob my head. "Understandable."

"I have no idea how we're going to get all of these people out of here." He glances around at the court overflowing with town residents.

"It's a good job I didn't marry you for your inability to blend in and take charge." Do I drop my voice and push in a little innuendo? Damn straight I do. Any incentive I can offer to get Colton to clear out the gymnasium so we can move tonight along, I'll make it.

Heat smolders in his gaze. I don't hold back my smirk.

"Put me to work, Coach." I tease the embers burning his gaze before I gasp. Colton's right there with me.

Shock ripples through me as cold water drenches my head, my clothes. Having closed my eyes at the onslaught, I blink them open, seeing Colton standing before me a soggy mess, his mouth gaping.

Mav and his teammates are laughing their asses off, holding on to two empty buckets, almost bent over as they struggle to contain themselves.

"Congrats on the win, Coach," my asshole son

says with a grin so damn wide, I've no choice but to mirror it.

Colton moves first, a damn sight faster than me as he loops his arm around Mav and hauls him close.

"Gah, no, you're wet."

"You think?" It's the only warning I give him as I lock him in tightly between me and Colton. The two of us hug him hard, taking great delight in his high squeals of complaint and laughter while his team-mates literally roll on the floor, laughing.

This here is everything I never dared to dream of or dared to wish for. Not only because wishing's for chumps, but because after Kelly, I thought I'd already been lucky in love. I didn't think it was possible to find enough room in my heart again for a love so strong.

But here we are, hugging our son and taking great delight in his laughter and the joy in his face. And as I hold on to Colton, I'm grateful for every second we've been gifted.

I HOPE YOU FELL IN LOVE WITH MY GUYS AND GOT swept up in the sweet escapism. If you're curious about Cass, Colton's good friend, we first meet him in my Zone Defense series. Check out book one, **No Take Backs**—though, a heads-up, we don't meet him until book three, **No Wrong Moves**. You can jump ahead as this is a stand-alone series.

Did you enjoy meeting Nash? The great news is, Nash has his very own sweet and sexy romance. Check out Collier's Creek book two, Elle Keaton's **Mandatory Repairs**.

ABOUT THE AUTHOR

I live and breathe all things book related. Usually with at least three books being read and two WiPs being written at the same time, life is merrily hectic. I tend to do nothing by halves, so I happily seek the craziness and busyness life offers.

Living on my small property in Queensland with my human family as well as my animal family of cows, sheep, chooks, and dogs, I really do appreciate the beauty of the world around me and am a believer that love truly is love.

To check for updates head to my website:
HTTPS://BECCASEYMOUR.COM
HTTPS://LANDING.MAILERLITE.COM/WEBFORMS/
LANDING/R9F0I4
Plus, join my Facebook group, which I share with the awesome Louisa Masters here:
HTTPS://WWW.FACEBOOK.COM/GROUPS/
ROMMANCEWITHBECCALOUISA/

facebook.com/beccaseymourauthor
twitter.com/beccaseymour_
instagram.com/authorbeccaseymour
bookbub.com/authors/becca-seymour
tiktok.com/@beccaseymourwrites